COME AWAY

COME AWAY

STEPHEN POLICOFF

DZANC
BOOKS

5220 Dexter Ann Arbor Rd.
Ann Arbor, MI 48103
www.dzancbooks.org

Designed by Steven Seighman

Cover painting: Richard Dadd. *The Fairy Fellers' Master-Stroke*. 1855–64. Oil on canvas. 54 x 39.5 cm.

Library of Congress Cataloging-in-Publication Data

Policoff, Stephen Phillip.
  Come Away / by Stephen Policoff.
    pages cm
  ISBN: 978-1936873609
  I. Title.
  PS3616.O566C66 2014
  813'.6—dc23

2014013183

First U.S. Edition: November 2014

Printed in the United States of America

10 9 8 7 6 5 4 3 2 1

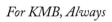

For KMB, Always

Come away, O human child!
To the waters and the wild
With a faery, hand in hand,
For the world's more full of weeping
than you can understand

—Yeats

COME AWAY

1.

Nadia called me a Zoloft dropout this morning and she wasn't smiling. That's no good. I need her smile—even the puzzled version, which is mostly what I see these days. When my lost-in-the-forest dreams hang down over me like black clouds and I leap up out of bed, gasping, Nadia's smile still calms me down. A little. It does.

I haven't told her about the dreams, really. I did tell her that Zoloft makes me feel like I am constantly coming down from some long drawn-out acid trip, but she just rolled her eyes. *You sound like my father when you say things like that,* she yelled at me once, and she's not somebody who yells very often.

"I don't get it," she said, packing up her cameras and equipment to head down to work. "Because you once told me, ages ago, that drugs were at the top of your list of *key life experiences.* I think you even used that phrase. So, now, when you need a different kind of life experience—when I need you, when Spring needs you to have a different kind of life experience—why can't drugs help you now?"

I winced when she said that name. Not a wince, really, just a little tic I've been noticing lately. A quick, tight pursing of the lips, like I'm trying not to speak. Or, I don't know, scream.

"It's not the same thing." I held the empty orange Zoloft bottle between two fingers like some disgusting tidbit of garbage I'd picked up off our floor. "That was about opening doors—doors maybe I don't want open anymore, but still, I don't mind that they were open once. This is more about closing doors, doors that maybe I'd like to be closed but not so hard, not so fast, not so completely."

She shrugged, never more beautiful than when mildly exasperated with me. "Try it again, maybe? For me? For Spring?"

I smiled as if I might actually do that, though it would involve retrieving the long white pills from the pile of brush and debris in the back yard where I tossed them the other night when my hand started shaking or felt like it was shaking and I couldn't sit down and I knew it was over between me and the Zoloft.

Nadia glides into our daughter's bedroom, looks down at her, bends over the jungle-themed toddler bed we bought at IKEA right before we moved out of the city.

She's stroking the wisps of her hair. I know that touch, that feathery touch; it's one of Nadia's sweetest gestures, but I can't help hissing, "You'll wake her up," though I know she won't. I would. I go in there sometimes just to look at her, just to check her breathing, and it's like she can sense the clumsy scrape of my shoes. Then big gray eyes pop open and she's staring at me, whispering, *Daddy?*

"It's okay," Nadia says, flinging on her black blazer. "She's sleeping like a baby."

"Except babies don't really sleep that well," I point out. "They whimper, they cough, they thrash."

"You never get tired of saying that, do you?" She smiles slightly, kisses me. "Don't forget to give her the meds. Don't let her climb too high, and if those nurses call again, try not to yell at them."

"I don't yell."

"Fine, just don't be so emphatic in telling them to go fuck themselves then."

She's about to dash out the door, late as usual for her commute down Route 28. I'm standing between her and the door, rooted like a tree. "Isn't your father supposed to be showing up today?" I ask, just to see if she will do what she always does when his name comes up, which is smack her forehead.

She does. "Shit! He is. Devoted grandpa. Amazing, isn't it? When I was Spring's age, I never saw him—he was always running off to Nepal or Ankara. Now we can't shake him." She laughs. She has this musical laugh I always enjoy. "Okay, I'll try not to be too late. I know how much you love bonding with my dad."

Actually, I have a question for her dad—a first, really—but I decide not to tell her this now, as she darts around me and bangs out the door, hops into the battered Subaru, speeds off down the hill.

I drift around the house, raising the blinds, looking out at the faint bluish light opening up above Simpson's Mountain. It's 5:30 AM, a time of day I used to see only from the other end of the night. Not that I was ever such a big all-night party boy, but I do remember one or two times, coming out of a club or a bar or someone's squalid apartment and the fact that it was dawn knocked me out. Where did it go? Where did that night go?

Now, the surprises are different, that small voice calling out in the early light for comfort, for security—things I've never been so good at providing.

I peek into her room. Her eyes are still shut tight, her tiny arms thrown back over her head like she was just dropped out of the sky. Her hair covers her face and does not look in the least bit green like I could have sworn it looked the other day, the day I stopped taking the Zoloft.

In the kitchen, I pour the dregs of the coffee into the heart mug that Nadia gave me last Father's Day; I look out at the mossy wooden bench that sits on the edge of our vast, leafy yard and suddenly I see something. Her again. A girl with greenish hair, sickly skin, darting under the bench and toward the thicket of bushes at the edge of the creek.

"Jesus!" I say, and I leap up, spilling coffee all over the counter.

"Daddy?" comes the small voice. My daughter is standing in the doorway, clutching her faded yellow duck, rosebud mouth in a yawn. "Did you see something out there?"

"No, sweetie. Nothing, nothing."

"Not the green girl?"

I shiver, furiously mopping up the coffee with an already filthy dishtowel.

"Uppy!"

I lift her up. She weighs nothing, nothing. But she's real. I have not imagined her, have not imagined the real weight of her—her life in my hands. I feel the back of her head, the still-fresh scar like a tiny ridge down the back of her fragile skull. I close my eyes to blot out the image of her falling but I can still see it.

When I open them again, she is gazing at me; she looks just like Nadia sometimes, has the same bemused smile.

"Do you…do you want your juice?" I manage.

"Juice!" she crows. "Then let's go outside. Let's look for the girl."

2.

I can't say being a father was ever high on my list. It made the list, sure—but somewhere above understanding the laws of physics and below learning to appreciate Cubism.

During my restless teen years, I actually liked kids, enjoyed their feral energy. As the Amazing Paul, I performed a vaguely competent magic act at birthday parties, forcing freshly scrubbed blond children to pick the nine of hearts then revealing that card attached to the head of a rubber snake; that always evoked a pleasing shriek from the six-year-old set.

But for all the years of my protracted young adulthood, the years of thrashing about, when I had no idea how to make my way in the world (which remains largely true but lost its urgency with the advent of Nadia, who knows well how to get on with things), having a kid was about as appealing to me as having dental work. Most days I could barely summon the will to shave, let alone spoon-feed a gurgling infant.

When I visited my sister June, who had wanted (and got) little more than a life as a Connecticut soccer mom, and saw how much energy it took even to get her daughter Morgan out the door, I shuddered. I pictured myself mired in endless, slow repetition of daily chores and I literally, visibly shuddered. "Is the house that cold?" June asked.

It was.

My first wife Laura and I were barely married long enough to water plants, much less have a child.

With my second wife, Annie, the story gets so convoluted I can't even tell it to myself anymore. We were (sort of) happy; we (accidentally) conceived a child. And this seemed as clear a message from the cosmos as I could imagine receiving. *You are not meant to have children. Do not have children.*

I remember what time it was: 6:06 PM. I can see that moment, frozen forever, as in a photo.

We were sitting in a booth at Captain Cass, a lobster joint in Rock Harbor, Cape Cod, not far from the crappy cottage where Nadia and I had just spent a disastrous, hurricane-swept vacation. The power had finally been restored across the Cape and we had cleaned up the mess in the cottage (though not in our relationship) and packed up our scattered and filthy belongings. It was not clear at that moment if we were going home to New York together or not.

It had been less than twelve hours since Nadia told me she was pregnant and I had said almost nothing about it. We sat there drinking iced tea, toying with onion rings. I picked at my fish and chips; Nadia devoured her lobster roll in seconds.

"I love this place," she said, after my lengthy discourse on how I was probably not supposed to be a father.

"Even today? With me?"

"Of course today, with you."

In the back of my every thought was a hum, a chant, like the voice of a hungry ghost: *You can't do this it won't work it will all go wrong it will come to nothing, nothing, nothing...*

My familiar anti-mantra, one I've listened to all my life, and pretty often it's proved accurate. Self-fulfilling prophecy? Or ineradicable life's truth?

"You decide," I muttered, as if Nadia were actually party to the conversation that was the soundtrack of my soul.

"I've already decided," she said. "Don't you know that by now?"

We walked out to Rock Harbor; it was only about 7:30 but the baleful late August sun was already starting to set. There was a lime-green boat bobbing out on the bay and a long-faced man sitting on deck, sunk in gloom, listening to his own dispiriting soundtrack. He looked like me.

"What?" I asked finally. "What have you decided?"

"That you will be a great father, that I don't want to do it without you, that things will be good, that we'll be happy…"

"I seem to lack the happiness gene," I said. "And I'm not sure I know how to be a good father since my own father was so locked up in himself that he never saw me for a minute, and what if I'm that way? I'm full of guilt and doubt; my favorite book is *The Trial*, for God's sake."

Nadia laughed. "*You're* a trial," she said. "But you're my trial." She stroked my hand, she looked out at the boats. "You *are* supposed to be a father. I can feel it. Don't you trust me? Don't you believe in me? Maybe that wasn't the baby you were supposed to have. Maybe this one is."

"Maybe. Maybe. Maybe that guy sitting there will get up, pour himself a big drink, and then jump into the bay and drown." I knew I was being tiresome and obtuse, knew it but couldn't stop myself. I was so used to dressing up in negativity that I felt naked, like the fabled emperor, if I started to shed that comforting cloak.

The long-faced man got up. He went below, came back with a shot glass full of what looked like absinthe—bright green, as green as his boat. He gulped it down and looked out over the bow. He smiled. A beatific beam, really. Right at us. At me. *Oh no*, I thought. *He really is going to jump.*

Then, for no apparent reason, he stuck out his tongue. At me. At us.

"Jesus," I said. "Let's go home."

"See?" Nadia said, slipping her arm through mine. "When we're together, things happen."

"Things happen." I sighed. "But that's dangerous, isn't it?"

"Maybe," she said. "For you."

3.

I never went for concept names. After my first marriage ended (mere moments after it began), I dated a girl named Bliss—*something we all crave*, she liked to say about herself, though her particular brand of mild hysteria was not what I craved.

When I drove over to her house to break up with her she gave me this startled look. "How can we break up?" she asked me, blue eyes gone grave. "We're not dating. We're not even really friends."

I've also known a very imprudent Prudence and a Melody who screeched when she spoke. And don't get me started about Christian Dove, my cousin Hank's daughter, named to honor the brief period (1975–6) during which this particular bonehead cousin joined Jews for Jesus, proselytizing crackpot theories throughout Scarsdale. Last time I heard about her, Chrissy, as she calls herself now, was running a Wiccan gift shop in Sedona.

Doesn't it seem, I don't know, risky to conjure up an emotion, a sensibility with your child's name, almost daring the law of unintended consequences to kick in?

So, when Nadia and I were trying to name our daughter, I kept pushing for old-fashioned names, down-to-earth names, like Jane and Anne and Elizabeth. Names with roots, history. But Nadia wanted something different—something special, she said, because we were going to be having a special daughter.

I was not authorized to even consider boys' names, because Nadia knew right away (well before her doctor casually let it slip) that this stranger coming into our lives would be a girl. Everyone said so—her maid of honor, Dakota, who's a doula (whatever that is) said so; her father, the new-age philosopher, said so. Even her mother said so, and her mother rarely says much of anything, at least to me.

"A daughter. Another girl in your life," she said to me, out of the blue, the morning of the slapdash wedding. "Will you disappoint her like Nadia's father did? Tell me that, Paul."

She didn't wait around for my reply—I'm sure she thought she knew the answer. She just drifted upstairs, obsessively twisting and untwisting her long black hair.

Okay, she wasn't too happy about Nadia marrying me, or about the fact that Nadia was four months pregnant when we got married, or that I am fifteen years older than Nadia, or that I was married twice before and have been known to do battle with inner demons and not always win. That part she must understand a little, I guess, since she's been in and out of expensive psychiatric facilities all of Nadia's life.

Nadia's mother, Pearl—see? a concept name again—was the cosseted daughter of a Chinese classical pianist, born and reared in Hong Kong. But her life in the U.S. was knotty and grim, and Nadia often says she brought her mother up, not the other way around. She has a low, sad voice, the same plaintive notes played over and over no matter what else is going on around her.

A few months later, as we paced the waiting room of the NYU obstetrics ward, Pearl fixed her beautiful black eyes on me and murmured, "There is an old Chinese expression you will need to know, Paul. *A daughter is a needle in the heart.*"

"What isn't?" I asked.

Pearl didn't have any preferences about our daughter's name; mostly she seems to have no preferences of any kind. But Nadia favored That Kind of Name: Harmony, Unity, Eternity. Her father suggested—as he usually did—that we imbibe mythos. "Here's my list," he offered, though no one could recall asking for his list. "Isis, Titania, Mab, Iseult…"

But I cut him short. "How about one of the Four Horsemen of the Apocalypse?" I suggested. "Famine, maybe."

Even my mother got involved in the name game. She's been living in Palm Beach, surrounded by the remnants of her bridge group from Portsmouth. They eat the same little chicken salad sandwiches they ate back in New Hampshire and have the same conversations they've always had, except that sometimes they talk about people who have been dead for decades like they're standing right next to them.

She couldn't make it up to our wedding—granted, it was my third, and she had no real reason to think this one might turn out any better. But she wanted to be involved in naming the unborn child of the wife she had not yet met. "Tell your wife that your father would really have liked it if the baby was named Miriam, for his beloved great-aunt. He always used to say that if we had a daughter we should name her Miriam."

"You did have a daughter," I pointed out. "My sister…June?"

"Oh. Her. Well, that was before he started saying it."

I never heard a word from my father about a beloved Aunt Miriam, but then my father rarely spoke to me except to express disapproval. Perhaps he sensed that silence and our guilty estrangement were the only ways he would have an influence on my life.

As the long winter dragged by, Nadia and I still had no name for this special daughter who would soon change everything. Each night we would read aloud from one of the vast tomes sent to us by friends and family with titles like *Name Your Baby and Shape Her Life*, *Heraldic Names for Your Young Hero or Heroine*, *The Jane Austen Name-the-Baby Book*. It was like in the story of Rumpelstiltskin, when the queen tries to guess the little man's name.

"Gisella?"

"Too airy."

"Persephone?"

"We're not Greek."

"Fanny?"

"Oh please!"

This was a not completely untenable way to avoid thinking about all the other unanswered questions of our marriage. (Where would we live? How would we live? Were we not completely and utterly unsuited to raise children together?)

The matter was finally resolved when, on the evening of March 21, after Chinese takeout in our cramped living room, Nadia emerged from the bathroom and said, "Call Dakota, call Mom, let's go, my water just broke," calm as calm.

I dropped my plate of orange chicken. "Now?" I gulped.

She picked up the little suitcase that had been sitting next to the kitchen for a week, and on the way out the door grabbed our Cape Cod Storm Scenes calendar from the refrigerator.

"Look!" she said. "It's the equinox today. Spring. Let's call her Spring."

So we did.

4.

The ill-named Bliss, by the way, was by no means the zenith of my romantic desperation. And in addition to the long list of women I regret having slept with, there is an equally long list of women I regret *not* having slept with. Shakily atop that list sits Siobhan, whom I circled around—we circled around each other, really—in the gray years between my instant divorce from Laura and my second marriage.

Siobhan was a bartender/flutist; she played with downtown music stars like Lamont Young, John Zorn, Shadow & Dream Ensemble. Our schedules barely coincided and we never shared much more than a weekly lunch date, some electric conversations, some persuasive kisses. She had a seven-year-old daughter and sleeping with her was too complicated to even think about, though I did think about it over and over.

I was still young and it seemed to me then that if you had to think about doing something that much, there was no point in actually doing it. Weren't love and sexual connection meant to spout out like a flume from a fountain?

One raw March afternoon at Ollie's Noodle Shop on upper Broadway, I said, "You are the most interesting person I know, but you are surrounded by hurdles and I don't think you really want me to jump over them."

She smiled, said nothing. That was our last lunch.

For years after that, I thought, *I could have loved her, she could have loved me.* And maybe that's true—maybe if I had managed to weave my way down her obstructed path my life might have opened up to brighter possibility sooner instead of tunneling deeper into some dark annex of the mundane.

Maybe.

Years later, Siobhan wrote me a note on thin cream-colored paper. The letters were elegant, neat, like a Catholic schoolgirl's cursive. All it said was, *You were wrong about me.* I didn't know what she meant. But I was well on the way to my catastrophic marriage to Annie by then, and it didn't seem to matter.

After that marriage finally whimpered to a close, I wondered if maybe marriage, any commingling of lives, *should* be something you do hesitate about, something you do circle around. Something you dip your toe into before plunging all the way in. Something you flounder around in like a swimmer worrying how far out into the lake he should go. That maybe the obstacles and improbabilities are supposed to be there, supposed to slow you down.

Maybe.

Or is that just more of my personal brand of labyrinthine doubt? Certainty is not my forte, as my many exes would surely agree, while wondering wishing worrying are as comfortable to me as an old suit (and all of my suits are old).

Nadia has no patience for my endless musing. She ignored this well-worn personality trait from the moment we met, and had already moved most of her possessions into my apartment on West 83rd Street before I actually noticed. I did keep one metaphorical eye on the door for the first several months we lived together; not that I had any plans to leave that hellhole—I had been living there seven years by then. Still, I kept murmuring to myself, even practicing sometimes the phrase *This isn't working out.*

Only it was. Slowly, gradually, like ice melting, I found instead the phrase, *Things are okay, things could be worse, they have been worse, they aren't worse now* seeping into my consciousness.

And even when I tried to shut out the words, I still heard the music. I tried badgering Nadia about it, since self-deprecation is the little raft I have long clung to.

"Why would you want to be with one of the walking wounded?" I demanded.

We were drinking beers in my—by then our—thumbprint of a kitchen. We were listening to some Celtic fiddle tunes emanating from the clunky brown radio on top of the refrigerator.

"Who knows?" she said cheerily. "Because you're funny?" She slid her small hand up and down the green bottle unselfconsciously. "And you make me feel beautiful? And sometimes things just work even if you can't say why?"

Not in my experience, I started to say. But she just turned up the volume on the radio and we swayed slightly to the hypnotic waves of fiddles, pipes, harps. Then she kissed me. And I felt her heart beating against me. Oh, I thought. *This is how it all starts.*

5.

"What's wrong with you…are you backsliding about her name?" Nadia asked me yesterday morning. "You told me you were okay with it, and she's five years old now—we can't change it, for God's sake."

I was shaking off the remnants of another lost-in-the-forest dream. My hands were trembling slightly and I was trying to pour coffee without looking like I had Parkinson's. "What are you talking about?"

But I knew. Nadia notices things—things I do, things I say—even when I don't notice them myself.

"You haven't called our daughter by her name in days," she said. "You hate that name."

But I like that name. I grew to like it, so clearly apt for the little sprite that she is. She has unearthly gray-green eyes with an ever so slight elongation, an echo of Nadia's half-Asian ancestry, wispy black hair with a reddish tinge, and her mouth bows upward so that even when she's sad she seems to be smiling, a quirk of physiognomy that everyone who meets her notices.

A little slip of a thing, always leaping and spinning around, springing up as if to announce *I'm here!* But four and a half weeks ago she almost wasn't here, and with my eyes shut in the hospital chapel while Nadia choked out a prayer, I could not picture her face. And ever since then I've been worried so worried that she won't be here the next time I look, and I think that's why I have not been able to say her name.

Spring Spring SpringSpringSpring

There. I can say it and she's still here, isn't leaving me, won't be taken away.

Right now she's bouncing up and down in her green booster seat, gulping down a bowl of allegedly healthy cereal, though the little whole grain rings are colors not found in nature and when I pop a couple in my mouth they have the strange dead taste of day-old honey. "Do I have school today?" she asks between mouthfuls.

"You do. And you're not even dressed. Come on, imp child. Let's get moving."

"Yay! 'Cause I told the girl to meet me there," she says, flinging off her flowered nightgown in the middle of the kitchen. She runs giggling into her room to get dressed and I follow.

"Do you know where Mommy left the magic cream?" Her room—more like a picturesque cell, really—is so strewn with toys, stuffed animals, books, and beads that sometimes objects seem to disappear, only to be found days later underneath a doll's hat.

She hands me the tube, and I gently rub a little onto the back of her tiny head, covering the angry red scar I can hardly bear to look at more than a month afterward.

"Did you take your medicine?"

"My capsooool?" she says. "Yeah, but the girl says I don't need it anymore."

"Then let's rock and roll." I grab her around her tiny waist and fling her over my shoulder, heading toward the car and the quick drive to Puck's Hill Preschool.

"Lunchbox, Daddy! Backpack, Daddy!"

"You're just like your mom," I say, not for the first time. "She never forgets anything either, even if I really, really want her to."

"What did you give me for lunch?"

"Chicken, carrots, grapes. Good?"

"Girl says I get the best lunches."

I leave her wriggling on my shoulder and fling her Tinkerbell lunchbox into her panda knapsack.

"Is this some new friend you keep talking about? What about your best buddy, Aidan?"

"Gone," she says, a little sadly.

"Gone where?"

But she's not listening to me. She's singing along to WDST's Grateful Dead Hour in the back seat. *"And it's just a box of rain, I don't know who put it there..."*

We cruise across the Woodland Valley Bridge. The creek is a brown torrent from the end-of-May downpours but the rhododendrons along Esopus Avenue are suddenly in full magnificent bloom, preternaturally purple and scarlet blossoms bobbing their little heads.

"Look at those flowers, Spring." There. I've said her name again. I can. I will. "Aren't they amazing?"

"Such a long, long time to be gone and a short time to be there..."

A steady stream of parents and kids heads up the long driveway to the school. "Which one is your friend?" I ask. I am struggling, as I do every day, to free her from the shoulder strap on her overly fussy car seat.

"Look, there she is, Daddy."

But she's not pointing to the big red door of the school; she's pointing to the crest of the hill below the school, where there are two scrawny horses tied to a fenced-in shack, and what looks like a small green girl—like something from my dream, like the girl in our yard—dashing just across the periphery of my vision.

"Hi, Girl!" she shouts. "Can I come with you later?"

6.

All my life I've had bad dreams. Both of my ex-wives relied on various tranquilizers, melatonin, and earplugs to build a zone of stillness around themselves as I tossed and heaved.

My night terrors impressed even my lifelong friend Tommy, whose massive drug use induced recurring hallucinations before it finally killed him. During the six months that he was my freshman roommate, I would occasionally lurch awake to see him sitting on the folding chair next to my bed.

"Never saw anybody sit up in bed screaming the way you do," he would murmur. "Except maybe me, sometimes."

Only Nadia—who can slip into deep sleep seconds after her head hits the pillow—seems immune. When I started having my lost-in-the-forest dreams, I asked her if she was noticing anything different about me, any disturbing night behavior.

She looked at me as if I were speaking in riddles (which, admittedly, I do sometimes). "It's not surprising you're having bad dreams, if that's what you mean," she said, bouncing out of bed to check our daughter's breathing. "But that kind of stuff, you know, that's what my father always talks about. I tune it out. Dreams. They just don't mean much to me."

I wish I could tune it out.

A permeable consciousness leading to paraphilia, her father calls it. It was the subject of one of his rambling articles (*Redemption Magazine*) right around the time our baby was born. Not that I often pay attention to the astonishing flow of books, essays, and oracular pronouncements he cranks out, but now and then his crackpot ideas do ring a bell for me.

"I call it the *swinging door effect.* Research suggests that some personalities incline toward a kind of swinging door between states of consciousness, so that the distinction between what is perceived during REM sleep and that which we believe we see with our day-to-day eyes is, shall we say, blurry." He gestured vaguely in my direction. "Mr. William Blake saw angels in a tree," he pointed out, slipping further into his lecture mode. He dandled his granddaughter on one bony knee, beaming furiously at her but not, it seemed to me, really looking at her. "Considered mad in his day, schizophrenic in ours. But perhaps those angels were merely dream objects seeping out into the daily world, hmmm? And this happens, it does. It happens not just to poets but to nobodies too. Society blames drugs or nervous breakdowns or post-traumatic stress, but possibly these are experiences of a seepage from one state of consciousness to another. Do you see what I mean, Paul?"

I didn't at the time, and I'm not sure I do now. But the swinging door image—sometimes I do feel like I live inside that swinging door. And this girl, this green girl I see sometimes, have seen since Spring's incident, I'm hoping this girl is just a dream object seeping into daylight.

If things go as I'd like this evening—and let's face it, they rarely do—I might get around to asking Dr. Maire for his opinion about this.

That I still call him Dr. Maire five years after marrying his daughter says something, I suppose. But to call him Eric just doesn't work for me. The man is a walking dissertation, immensely learned about subjects few care about (the cult of Osiris in late Victorian London, the use of sacred mushrooms in pre-Roman Gaul) yet classically clumsy with human connections. He had been mostly out of Nadia's life since she was six, when he left for a conference in Bali and never returned. He's been married and divorced at least four times since then. Nadia claims to have lost count. But our own wedding seemed to stir something in him—do I dare call it fatherliness?

He almost wasn't invited. Nadia, among the most decisive of women, could not resolve the old *should I let him walk me down the aisle?* dilemma. She had seen him exactly three times in the previous five years, and her mother's jaw still visibly tightens at the mention of his name. Yet Nadia still cared about him—a vivid demonstration of the truth that men rarely deserve the love we receive. So, she decided to walk down the aisle alone but invited her father to the wedding under strict instructions that he was not to speak or even make eye contact with her mother. (Not such a great burden to place on him; he rarely makes eye contact with anyone, too busy looking inside himself, I suppose.)

He arrived wearing some sort of beige linen jungle explorer outfit; he was affectionate, expansive. He vowed to visit us often. Nadia just rolled her beautiful eyes, having heard such protestations all her life. But since then he's made a somewhat unnerving habit of showing up at our place—first in our tiny New York apartment and even more frequently since we moved to Ulster County. He gazes at Nadia fondly, heaves little sighs suggesting that he knows he failed her; he gives piggyback rides to his gleeful grandchild and demands that we let him take us out to dinner at La Duchesse Anne in Mt. Tremper, one of his former haunts. That we usually end up reheating old pasta while he drinks many glasses of my wine does not wholly detract from the thrill of his actually thinking about something as mundane as dinner.

The phone rings, and I freeze, always afraid bad news will insert itself into even the quietest of my mornings. But it's Nadia, calling from work.

"You're supposed to call, report on how Spring was this morning. Remember me, the mom?"

"Lovely. She was lovely. Laughing, happy, ate her breakfast, eager for school. Do you know anything about some green girl who's her friend?"

"Some girl named Green?"

"No. Some girl who is green."

"Like she wears a lot of green?"

"No. Her skin. Her hair. They're sort of green."

"Green?" There is a funny clicking sound on the other end of the phone. "Like, sickly looking? What do you mean?"

"Nothing. Just something I dreamed, I think. How's the magazine? How's your morning going?"

"Fine," she says, slowly, not fine at all.

7.

We did at least get a trip to London out of my father-in-law's newfound enthusiasm for family.

I've never quite grasped how Dr. Maire became a one-man panel of experts on all things paranormal, but he's always working on three different books, lecturing at this or that conference, being interviewed by obscure magazines (*The Fortean Times, Shadow & Psyche, Entheogenic Experiments Today*).

In April, one of his former students, now the curator of Pre-Raphaelite paintings at the Tate Museum, invited him to give a lecture as part of some conference on Folkloric Iconography in Victorian Paintings. She also offered him her empty flat in Putney, and, in possession of many frequent flier miles from his years of evading ordinary life, he called Nadia, begged her to have the whole darn family join him on this jaunt.

"Don't you think Spring is a little too young to attend an academic conference?" I asked him, when Nadia passed me the phone.

"My boy, you must relinquish your grasp on that elf child!" he said. "If I can do anything for her it will be to open the door to her journey, to introduce her to whole new worlds. This would be a start."

I try not to journey anywhere. And new worlds don't appeal to me much; I have enough trouble with this one. But Nadia spent a year in London when she was four—right before her parents' marriage dissolved—and I could tell right away she wanted to go.

"I could take awesome London-in-the-April-rain pho-tographs for a calendar or something," she whispered in one ear while Dr. Maire exhorted me in the other. "Spring would love Kensington Gardens! You could do research on that crazy painter you talk about."

So, okay, I said we'd go, though I saw the faint glimmer of doom out of the corner of one eye.

"Oh, you always see that," Nadia laughed when I mentioned this to her later. Though maybe she wouldn't laugh so much about it now, after the incident.

An eight-hour flight with a five-year-old is no one's idea of a vacation. But even I had to acknowledge that the transatlantic trip went pretty smoothly. Spring was happy, burbling; she lis-tened to the tapes her grandfather had sent her (a strange mix of Fairport Convention, Queen, and Jerry Garcia), watched var-ious versions of *Peter Pan*, her current favorite, on the portable DVD player; she hummed along with the music, drew elaborate pictures of trees and flowers, ate at least two bags of pretzels, slept.

The flat was a short walk through a churchyard to a rustic pub, the Beltane Arms, where Dr. Maire regaled us with lager, fish and chips, and a vast, lime-colored creamy mess called the Beltane Fool, which almost sent my daughter into a sugar-in-duced frenzy.

Nadia believes in the forced-march approach to touring, so we must have hiked about thirty miles through the city that first blurry day. The Chelsea Embankment! Speaker's Corner! Trafalgar Square! We alternated chasing the kid and carrying her on our backs or over our shoulders, though like her mother she is close to the textbook definition of indefatigable. Not me. I wilt at the mere suggestion of a trek. But I did enjoy the Sir John Soane Museum with its admirable mélange of Hogarth prints and historical gewgaws, and the statue of Peter Pan in Kensington Garden elicited a loud yay! from my sweet, jetlagged child.

Spring. Say it again. Spring.

Nadia skipped Dr. Maire's lecture the next day and took a train to Bath with Spring. But I spent hours at the Tate, gazing at the solemn, beautiful-yet-goofy Burne-Jones paintings of aesthete knights and feverish damsels, at the chic drowned Ophelia, and especially at the transfixing weirdness of *The Fairy Feller's Master-Stroke* by Richard Dadd, a tiny painting I had wanted to see for fifteen years.

Nadia calls photography her life's work, but that phrase has never meant much to me. My life's work seems to be just getting through my life, but I do have my little fixations, my pet projects. I had recently ditched one old project that had threatened to veer out of control, but this blank spot in my psyche was quickly filled by the return of my interest in the unspeakably strange Victorian artist Richard Dadd, who spent much of his life in a mental hospital painting Bosch-like scenes of his hallucinatory life. I took some art history courses in college (in my nonstop efforts to postpone pragmatic decisions) and now and then I've thought I'd be good at writing one of those baroquely illustrated think-books you see in museum gift shops, about painting and delusion, nightmare and symbol. Except, of course, that I know nothing much about these things and have no real qualifications to write about them.

But I could not take my eyes off this painting, could not stop the monologue in my mind about this painting. I had seen reproductions many times, but the eerie perspective, the almost three-dimensional details whispered to me from the canvas, beckoning me.

I felt faint. I felt foolish. I tried to focus on the central image of the painting, the "fairy feller" himself, a figure with a giant ax about to cut a hazelnut in half. Yet the sinister green faces of all the eerie peripheral figures kept summoning me, leering at me.

"Fascinating, yes, Paul? That you and I share an interest in mad Dadd," Dr. Maire said, slipping up behind me. "Do you know the poem he wrote about this painting? *In a dark green wood/In a misty dew / Shall we let him split the one into two?* Devilishly twisted stuff. Some say Dadd was in a cult of Osiris, a sort of murderous Theosophy spin-off. Some say this painting can be read as an allegory of the unconscious, or as the result of ergot poisoning, or as the true picture of the world perceived by an illuminated adept, virtually vibrating with chthonic creatures most of us can't see. What do you think?"

"I think it's time for tea," I said.

The lecture itself—which contained word for word the sentence he had rehearsed in my presence—was "stimulating indeed," according to the London Times. I didn't hear so much of it, trying instead to recall a line from Dadd's somewhat incomprehensible poem, a poem I had read twenty years before. *With a something axe he somethings his thumb but the something is not now it is yet to come...*but I was tired and jumpy and could not conjure the words.

I closed my eyes while Dr. Maire droned on, but even then I saw Dadd's faery world, still saw the ominous insect-like faces, the jeering greenish figures I think I have seen sometimes in my dreams, and I kept seeing them until polite applause brought me back to the folding chair, the lecture hall, the beaming, donnish crowd.

In the gift shop, Dr. Maire signed copies of his latest tome. I bought a book called *Visions of the Faery World*, which featured beautiful reproductions of the paintings coupled with an opaque text about Victorian metaphysics.

That night, back at the flat, I showed Spring some of the magnified details from the Dadd painting—the insect woman, the glowering goblin. I'd imagined her eyes wide with a five-year-old's fascination with the images. Instead she shrieked, "Do not like that place! Do not like that man!" She shook her little head at the green faces, swatting the pages as if they were flies, cried and cried and rubbed her eyes with balled-up fists, as if to blot out what she had seen.

"What the hell were you thinking?" Nadia kept asking me as she paced up and down the hallway all night, patting Spring's sweaty head, trying to soothe her onto the cot we had set up for her in the living room. "Do you want her to be even more like you, seeing things that aren't there?"

"She's nothing like me," I said. "And I don't see things that aren't there. I don't."

But the words sounded tentative, even to me, and as I looked out the window at the gray London dawn, at the magpies and foxes racing and twittering through the nearby churchyard, I wondered for a moment if I had any idea—now or ever—what I was seeing.

8.

I am staring down at the sea-green bed of the phone, wondering where the receiver could be. Spring often takes the phone to her room for pretend-to-be-Mommy games, carrying on gibberish arguments with imaginary editors. But the receiver was nestled snugly in its little bed when I ferried Spring to preschool this morning (three hours ago; three more to go before I pick her up). No one but me has been in the house—I think! I believe!—so where is the phone?

It's not that I am craving telephonic connection—I could go weeks without picking up that intrusive object—but I have a vague memory that the nurse I told to go fuck herself said she would be calling again today (Thursday, May 30) and it would probably be better for us all if I did not have to fling things around the room to find the receiver, could instead speak calmly and rationally into it. If I could speak calmly and rationally.

I have already straightened up the mess in various corners, the piles of clothes, magazines, bills, bags, toys which forever threaten to engulf my life. No phone.

Both Nadia and Spring are from the scattered-possessions school of living. I frequently find Nadia's socks, bras, and gum wrappers wedged into the couch. Spring sometimes leaves a trail of stuffed animals from the front door to her bedroom. I follow along behind both of them, sighing and picking things up.

"You don't know how to clean anything," my first wife asserted during our minutes-long cohabitation. "But you are insanely neat."

I think which of us was insane is open to debate. (Was I the one, for instance, who went down on our neighbor while her husband dozed in the next room?) But it is true that I barely noticed the brackish moldy rings in the bathtub of that rundown Connecticut condo, while the smallest pile of slightly askew mail on the dining room table compelled me to whisk it away to my unused desk.

Possibly the phone is in the laundry hamper. Nadia once absentmindedly tossed it there along with the shirt she had been wearing when baby Spring spit up on her shoulder while she was in mid-chat with Pearl. Nadia is only intermittently absentminded (childcare is the great equalizer, I guess), while I am ploddingly absentminded on a daily basis. I often stride purposefully into a room only to freeze with the sudden insight that I can't recall what propelled me there. I routinely write lists of things we need, tasks in want of performing, then realize that I've misplaced or tossed out the list.

At times I fear early Alzheimer's—but no, my sister told me, in one of our rare telephone conversations. "No, Paul! You were always like that. You lost your first paycheck, you lost your high school diploma. Dad always said it was your single worst trait."

My father often listed traits of mine that annoyed him. I was not aware he had a favorite.

The phone is not in the laundry hamper but lots of Spring's filthy clothes are: her FOREVER WOODSTOCK t-shirt has what looks like an entire bowl of peas smeared onto it; her striped skirt is caked with the remains of mint chocolate chip ice cream; there are grass stains on all three pairs of her jeans, which are tangled together as if they were mating. Okay, then—phone or no phone, I'll do some laundry.

What did I do, I sometimes wonder, before Nadia, before Spring? How did I fill up the long, uncentered days?

Being productive at work, is what I wish I could say. Having fun, making love to beautiful women, toasting the manifold joyous moments of this world.

Well, there were a few bursts of such activity (not so much the toasting; I was never good at celebrating, or even unearthing, joyous moments). But mostly I did what I still do, which is nothing much. Doing nothing has always been my strongest skill.

I watch—or appear to watch—the news. I listen to WDST, though half the time I come to consciousness at the end of an eight-song medley and wonder what I have been listening to. I walk down to the bridge. I stare at the screeching teens tubing the Esopus or the placid kayakers or the family of ducks serenely paddling down the creek. I walk to the tiny Phoenicia library and read faint copies of articles from art history journals obtained for me by the beaming librarian ("Victorian Fairy Paintings: Aesthetic or Psychoactive?") and pretend that I might actually work on my little Richard Dadd project. I drive to the Boiceville Supermarket trying, usually in vain, to find food that will not evoke Nadia's hyper-parental ire. I transport Spring to and from preschool, play dates, or the Y in Kingston for Tadpoles Free Swim (which isn't free).

Most of these things do not need to be done at the exact moment I am doing them; many don't need to be done at all. Like this load of laundry which, having brought down into the dank basement, I leave on top of the dryer muttering, "Later."

The phone rings, as it has to, and I dash back up the cement steps, kicking at cushions and sweaters, hoping to find it. I am in mid-whirl when I spot it next to the kitchen sink—how did I not see it there before?—and grab it, thinking, Okay, nurses, what now?

But it is Jack, shouting, "Brickner! How goes it?" When I don't respond, he adds, "On my way over there! Need to talk!"

Typically, he does not ask if it is okay for him to barge into my life.

"Oh," I say, clicking my teeth like a crazy person "Oh. Sure."

9.

Jack says becoming a father made him want to work even harder than before. "For them. Make the world new. Every morning I wake up like lightning struck the bed—bam! I am out of there and all I want to do is work, work, work," he tells me.

I admit this has not been my experience. After my daughter was born, I stopped working altogether. I think more but do less—although, as Nadia sometimes likes to ask, "How could you think more? How could you do less?"

But Jack was always a cartoonish action figure. He can't stay still even when he's sitting in my living room, trying to tell me a story about his sons and some kind of education center around here where he wants to bring them.

Jack is another reason I'm no longer working. He was my boss for seven years, a trust-fund rich kid and the publisher of mostly dull-as-paint business journals, like *Plumbing Fixtures Today*, *Pressure Vessel Technology*, and *The Journal of Impression Management* (my own bête noire). Sure, he was my friend, too, more or less—my drinking/substance abuse buddy, anyway. But always he enjoyed playing the boss, taking real pleasure in shouting, "Brickner, that last issue wasn't up to your usual! I want you to do better!" or "Brickner, I want you to rock the world of PR with your next column!"

And I did. For seven years, I did. I made *The Journal of Impression Management* an almost interesting magazine. And I was committed to it, more or less, the way you get committed to a job that is not especially engaging but not utterly despicable either. But when Nadia and I realized we could not stay much longer in our tiny Manhattan apartment (or let's say that Nadia realized and made sure that I came to realize it too) and we decided more or less on a whim to leave New York for the verdant hills of Ulster County, the idea of commuting back down to the city to perform work that had not once filled my heart with anything but apathy made my commitment plummet like a balloon leaking air.

And it was Jack who made it all seem right. "New marriage, new child, new home!" he blared at me when, two days before the moving van showed up, I finally got around to telling him I was leaving the city. "That calls for a new plan, Brickner. A whole new work plan, a whole new life plan."

Except I was never good at having a plan of any kind, much less a new one. So Nadia came up with one instead. She shed her freelance photographer role like a costume that had never fit her, strode into the offices of *Ulster Magazine* in somnolent uptown Kingston, New York, and skipped out ten minutes later as their new photography editor.

"You take care of Spring for a few years, work on your weird projects, and I'll make some money," she assured me later that day. "When we get sick of this routine, we'll swap."

It had only been a week since we moved into the blue house just past the Woodland Valley Bridge in Phoenicia, about half an hour from Kingston. I was in our newly painted kitchen, microwaving the organic sweet potato goop that was Spring's favorite lunch at the time (she was ten months old, already burbling and crawling and pulling herself up on chair legs and cruising around unpacked boxes and crates in the living room, trying to walk). I dipped a finger into the bowl, testing it to see if it was too hot. I scalded my finger, dropped the bowl, cursed.

"Don't you think I'm, I don't know, not so well equipped for that role?" I managed.

Nadia laughed. "No, goofball, I think you're perfect for that role. You have a gift for devotion. It's not a very well-wrapped gift, but it's a gift just the same." And she kissed me, and thus it was decided.

A few months later, Jack called me up, bellowing into the phone, "We're following your lead!"

I had no idea what he meant, was briefly fearful that he meant he was moving to Phoenicia (because, though I like Jack, I also like not to see him very much). But he didn't mean that, he meant he and Gwen were having a kid (twin boys, as it turned out). Within weeks, he had sold his business and the new family moved up to Delmar, a suburb of Albany, Gwen's hometown, where Jack now publishes medical textbooks. And ever since then he's called me once a week, asking for childcare tips, talking a mile a minute about his new, quieter lifestyle, the strange thrill of being a father, the extraordinary pleasure that little Henry and Edward bring him, saying we have to get together to compare notes.

Okay, I say. Sure, any time.

Except maybe not now.

Because in a couple of hours, I have to pick Spring up from nursery school, and then there's the whole Dr. Maire visit thing, and my plan to quiz him about seeping dream objects before Nadia shows up. But Jack has it in mind to tell me something, something he deems important. I know this because he isn't actually making any sense right now, and that's always a sign that something's on his mind.

Once, back when we were still going out on the town every night, he stopped by my apartment with a thermos of mint juleps (his family was originally from Virginia). He was already loaded, and with no introduction he started listing all the women he had ever slept with and what had been wrong with each one. Mostly, it turned out, they had not smiled enough, they worried, they sweated, they strained, they were fake, they were all hair and breasts, they wore the wrong clothes, they didn't wear enough clothes, they looked better in clothes than out of clothes, they did not go to the right school, they had not learned the right lessons, they had learned their lessons too well.

They were human, in short, and I had no idea where this conversation was going until he began to sob. "That's why I have to marry Gwen," he said. "I can't find anything wrong with her! I've tried, too! But the way she smiles at me, Brickner, like I'm the sun and moon to her. How can I say no to that? How can I not marry her?"

Freshly wounded from my second marriage, at the time, I wanted to say, *How can you not marry her? Let me count the ways!* But I didn't. I took a swig out of the thermos, that he (finally) passed me. I passed it back, laughing an utterly false laugh.

"To Gwen!"

"To Gwen!" he roared. He fell back onto my couch, spilling the rest of the bourbon down his stone-colored polo shirt.

Well, I owe him a lot, as he likes to point out—it was at his wedding that I met Nadia, a distant cousin of Gwen's hired as their photographer. I still smile when I remember her racing about the restored Dutch mansion where the wedding was held, trying to capture the joy and spontaneity not especially on view at this event. So for that reason, and for all the other reasons we tolerate the inexplicable passions of our friends, I am trying to figure out what it is that he is getting at, while keeping half an eye on the clock in the kitchen.

I do notice that Jack seems to have gained some weight, looks a little more rumpled. This is a man whose khakis were previously so well pressed they looked starched, his thinning yellow hair always combed with a neat, schoolboy part.

"Because suddenly they seem different to me—I can't put my finger on it. They don't laugh, they don't smile, they look out into space, they don't seem to hear me. Maybe not both, maybe only Edward, or maybe it's just that he's worse or that he's the more beautiful of the two and so I notice more that his face looks wrong, changed. I can't tell, I can't tell. Do you worry about this, Brickner? About something happening to your kid that you can't understand, can't describe, can't even imagine?"

I shudder. I don't know if he notices it, but I do, my hand shaking like it shook the other night, the night I threw out the Zoloft. I'm thinking about my lost-in-the-forest dreams, about Spring's incident, the blood, the terrible scar. And the green girl I've seen calling to Spring, asking her to come away with her.

But it's almost time to pick her up, make sure she's still alive, still with us, still the sweet and lovely child whose every move is a pleasure and a torment to me. It's time not to think about things I can't see, or things I do see but can't name.

I shake my head. I shake it too hard—surely he can see that. "No," I say. I laugh just as I did the night he told me about Gwen, so mirthless anyone paying attention would notice. "No, I never worry about things like that."

10.

"This is your car?" Jack asks.

I jiggle the rusted door handle. "Okay, it's not a Mercedes." It is, in fact, the battered hulk of what was once a forest-green Taurus, the kind of car that lives in driveways and front yards all across Ulster County. "Nadia uses the good one for work. This one mostly goes back and forth to preschool."

Which is where I would be heading right now were it not for Jack's newfound interest in the psyche. It turns out that he has been having repeated dreams just like my lost-in-the forest dreams. He blurted this out as he was prodding me into this questionable expedition.

I have to say that I've never imagined Jack paying a lot of attention to his dreams. Once, years ago, at the Lion's Head, a downtown bar frequented by actual journalists where Jack used to hang out to make himself feel better about publishing *Pressure Vessel Technology*, we were drunkenly arguing about lust and why we want who we want, and he said, *I don't believe in any of that Freudian crap, I don't believe in the unconscious at all. The surface, baby, that's all there is to me and you.*

Well, to you anyway, I thought.

Of course, that could just be the sort of thing you say when you're drunk and twenty-eight. But it seemed so right at the time, that he would feel that way, that he lived his life that way, that on the seesaw of self-knowledge he was all the way up in the air, waving and shouting, while I was crouching on the ground, staring at my feet.

But he's different this time, more thoughtful maybe, which wouldn't be all that difficult, but still. I see doubt on his face where before I never saw anything but blue-eyed certainty. And he seems thirsty for details of my life rather than merely using me as a vessel into which he might pour his own.

Which wasn't at all what I expected or wanted from this afternoon. When I started looking obsessively at my watch— *About two hours till I have to pick up Spring. Only about a hundred minutes till I have to pick up Spring*—he said, "I'll go with you to pick up your daughter, but first we have to swing by this place, this center. You'll take me there, right?"

I nodded.

"I need to see this place. It's near here. Gwen doesn't approve, but I think it's what we need for the boys. We need a treatment, we need a plan, so take me there, Brickner."

This place, this center is on Pantherkill Road, about half a mile from our house, so I said okay, knowing Jack would not let go of this idea, would badger me about it the rest of the day until I complied.

We snake across a leafy road up a hill, past startled deer drinking from a little stream. The air is thick with the screeching of blue jays and frantic chipmunks, and ahead of us is a dark thicket of trees that makes me hit the brakes.

"Like a scene from my dreams," I mutter, and Jack immediately starts pestering me to tell him the dream. I shake my head, drive on.

We pull into a circular driveway surrounded by a series of small green buildings. A sign reads The Grunwald Neo-Changeling Center for Childhood Retrieval.

"This is the place," he says.

"What's a *neo-changeling*?" I ask.

We get out, and I'm feeling even more irritable than usual—the forest, the buildings: they're getting on my nerves. I have spent some unpleasant hours in strange healing centers over the years and this place feels way too much like other places I've been. The main office looks as if it were built out of logs, like a child's idea of a rustic cabin, but inside, over the front desk, is a gigantic reproduction of that painting, *The Fairy Feller's Master-Stroke*. My mouth falls open.

"Like it?"

A short, balding, bearded man sidles up to me. He's wearing a light green lab coat and looks as if he has just stepped out of an emergency room or a psych ward. His nametag reads DR. GRUNWALD, DIRECTOR.

"Given to me years ago by a famed scholar, a former colleague. So appropriate for this place because, you see, our motto here pace Dadd is, *We bring the hidden into view / We shall not let the one be split in two.*"

"Interesting," I whisper.

"Say it with me!" he exhorts. "*We bring the hidden...*"

"We came to see what you do here," Jack says loudly. He seems to be nudging me aside, as if I'm getting in his way. "Jack Donald. We spoke yesterday..."

Grunwald cuts him off. "I speak to many parents. So many worried parents these days. Can't really show you much of what we do, so sorry, not until we see your child, see what we can see about your child. A boy, is it?"

"Twins. They're four."

"And you've lost them, have you? They've changed? The boys you knew have slipped away somewhere? They've been, you almost think, replaced?"

Jack gasps. "Yes," he barely says. "Yes."

"Well then, bring the boys in, bring the wife, bring them all," Grunwald says, suddenly jolly. "Pleasure." he says to me, sticking out his thick hand. I shake it warily and he strides off down the green hallway, whistling a vaguely familiar tune.

We get back into the car. I sit there, staring at my Ganesha keychain (a gift from Dr. Maire, of course), as if I were not quite sure what to do with it.

"Strange strange but good good, don't you think, don't you get a good feeling from that place?" Jack burbles.

"Yes," I say. "No," I say. "No!"

I don't look at him.

"After Spring's incident I started having these dreams, every night, sometimes more than once a night. I'm in a forest, it's dark and I'm alone and Spring is lost and I can't find her and I hear her voice, I hear her crying, I hear her sob, *Daddy, Daddy, help me! Where are you?* Only I can't move, can't see. I want so much to see her face, just to see it, but I can only hear her crying louder and louder and sometimes there are these creatures, little dwarfish green figures like in that painting, like in that damn painting, and they're running all around me, scurrying like insects through the woods around me, and I want to scream but I can't or won't and I hear something else, I hear a thump a loud *thump thump*, like an ax, an ax chopping wood, and I wake up and my heart is pounding, and I am drenched in sweat, and that's all."

"You didn't tell me Spring had an...incident," he says, after a long moment.

"I didn't tell anyone."

We are still idling in the circular driveway. I'm having a hard time ridding myself of the image from Dadd's painting, the way those faces seem sometimes to be peering at me, right at me with their sinister eyes.

"I have dreams like that sometimes about my boys. No, really, I do. Lost. Them. Or me. Can't figure it out. That's why I'm thinking we have to try everything, we have to bring the boys here. Gwen says no. She says I'm losing it, I say I may have found it. She says I'm the one who's changed, not the boys, but if I am, I'm changed for the better! Let's go back inside, Brickner. Let's poke around here some more."

I glance at my watch. It's time to get Spring. I gun the engine. "Got to go."

We race down Woodland Valley Road toward Puck's Hill and I cannot find another word to say to Jack.

11.

Spring's teacher, Miss Tania, beams at me, her pale blue eyes blinking furiously. In another era of my life, I might have wondered if she were flirting with me. I was always particularly unskilled at picking up on these signals, almost always wrong when I imagined a woman sought my attention, or stunned afterward to discover that the woman I shrugged off as unattainable had a violent crush on me.

These days, I am too tired or distracted with worries about Nadia and/or Spring to care about such attention, though Miss Tania is hard to ignore. She is taller than I am, almost too thin, with wavy reddish hair pulled back into a nineteenth-century bun. She has the kind of complexion that makes the phrase *white girl* conspicuously clear. And she began loudly yoohooing me, striding in my general direction as soon as I walked in and scanned the avocado-colored playroom for my daughter.

"Your little Springlet is such a gift," she gushes.

I laugh. "She is a gift. Is she doing okay?"

"Imaginative, vivacious, thoughtful, oh my!" She has a not entirely discernible accent. Scottish? Australian? South African?

"I do believe she will be quite a vision in our little show next month. You will be coming, will you not?"

"Show?"

"Tableau Day, I like to call it. A masque. For our gala graduation day. We will have song, dance, some scenes from Shakespeare..."

"Shakespeare? In nursery school?"

"My adaptation, of course. Indeed, Mr. Brickner, Spring tells me that you write...books?"

"I wouldn't go that far."

"Perhaps...perhaps, you could be persuaded to go over our little script with me?" she twinkles. She is speaking directly to me, but she is not looking at me. Her eyes are darting all around the crowded room.

"I...don't think I can," I manage. "Where is Spring? I haven't seen her come in yet."

"Gamboling on our beloved hill, I would guess. And what of Mrs. Brickner? Will she be coming to our masque? One never sees her. Some of the staff believes you must be a single father. No?"

"No. Spring's mom works in Kingston. Why?"

"We are, some of us, just wondering if little Spring has, how to put this, proper guidance? Might she not be, perhaps, missing the sort of boundaries a mother's love might provide?"

I chew my thumbnail, trying hard to resist suggesting that Miss Tania might like to go fuck herself. I am hoping to avoid that suggestion. "You just told me she was imaginative, vivacious, and thoughtful."

"True. But I did not say grounded, did I? Don't get me wrong, Mr. Brickner, Spring is a joy. But a bit of a wild child, no? And one cannot help wondering who her influences are. And where the...lacunae?...may be."

"Her mother adores her and she has..."

"But was there not some hospitalization recently? Some untoward event?"

"She fell. She's fine."

"If you say so, Mr. Brickner." Miss Tania turns abruptly. She takes a pennywhistle out of her dress pocket and blows several reedy notes on it. "Children!" She waves one long arm. "Come to the circle. Time for goodbyes!"

"I don't see her little friend here anymore," I say, desperate to change the subject. "A boy named Aidan?"

Miss Tania's eyes go wide just for an instant. She shakes her head, either in sorrow or in consternation. "Poor dear boy. Issues. The Spectrum, some say. Not dealt with. Dangerous. Gone. Whisked away."

"Whisked away where?" I ask, but Spring comes bounding in from the playground, flushed and gorgeous. Her eyes light up when she sees me.

"Daddy, Daddy!"

"Not yet, Little Spring," Miss Tania chides, nudging her back toward the circle. "Goodbyes first, then hellos! Am I right, Mr. Brickner?"

"Sure," I say, not at all sure.

The children squeal and run around the green circle painted in the center of the floor. One of Miss Tania's assistants, who looks no older than eleven, begins to strum a guitar.

Miss Tania leans in to me, as if to a secret lover. "So, we will see you at the Great Event?" she asks. "And Spring's mother too?" She straightens up, extends her arms in some unclear supplication. "Yes, yes, Spring is a gift. But remember, Mr. B., that sometimes the trouble is not now, sometimes the trouble is yet to..." She whirls suddenly. "Children, sit!" she commands. She strides to the center of the room, and I am standing on the periphery as usual, looking very intently at my thumb.

12.

Spring bounces down the steps, flings open the door of our beat-up Taurus, barely gives a glance to the stranger in the front seat.

"Oh, you're even prettier than your daddy said," he declares. "Call me Uncle Jack!"

"You're not my uncle," she points out, then turns to me. "When is Pop-Pop coming? Want to see him! Want to tell him about my new friends."

Pop-Pop is what she calls Dr. Maire, whom she loves with a depth he almost certainly does not deserve. He seems the least Pop-Pop person I've ever met, but maybe my daughter has unearthed the Pop-Pop buried inside the philosophe.

"He could materialize at any moment," I tell her, as I struggle for the second time today with the strap on her car seat, trying to keep her secure, trying to keep her here, right here.

She falls asleep the instant the car moves, as she always does. Jack cranes his neck around and stares at her, at her sweet face, never sweeter than when she is in the momentary bliss of deep sleep.

"Tell me about the…incident. Was it a bad…incident?"

I gnaw my lip, nod.

"What happened?"

I shrug. "She was hurt. She could have died. I haven't been able to get that out of my head."

"What about the dreams? You're still having dreams about it? Recurring dreams. Isn't that what they call them? I have them too. Did I tell you this? Sometimes, I can't tell the difference anymore between what I've said and what I've thought. The boys snatched away from me. A giant hand. Don't they say a recurring dream must mean something, must be trying to teach us something?"

"They say a lot of things."

We pull up to the house. Dr. Maire's ancient Volvo is not there and I notice, as I did not before, that Jack's Mercedes is half on our lawn, half on Woodland Valley Road, as if he had been in such a hurry that he skidded to a halt and did not look back.

I scoop Spring up, light as air, carry her tiny sleeping form over my shoulder. I love the feel of her body on my body, her tiny hot breaths on the back of my neck.

Jack hesitates, watching me head to the house. I'm hoping he'll get the message for a change, that it's time, time for a shift in the day. He sighs loudly. I don't honestly think I've ever heard him sigh, so used is he to having things the way he wants them.

"Got to get home to Gwen and the boys, I guess," he says finally. "Am I imagining that they've changed? That something has been scooped out of them and all we have left is the shell? I don't think so. I don't think I'm imagining it. So, we'll be back here tomorrow. Yes, tomorrow. Got to bring Henry and Edward to see that man, find out what this Grunwald has to say. See you then?"

"Sure," I say halfheartedly, heading to the door, to safety.

He stands frozen in my driveway. "Brickner," he persists. "What do you think? What do you think those dreams are trying to teach you? And if I was actually having dreams like that, just say I was, what would they be trying to say to me?"

"That it's better not to fall asleep sometimes," I say.

He laughs, thinks I'm joking.

13.

Nadia says Spring looks a little under the weather, but I don't see it. Under the weather seems a strange way to describe someone as energetic as Spring, though her coloring does look a little off. I never paid much attention to her coloring until the incident. She normally has a slightly paler version of Nadia's ivory skin; when she's tired or excited or hurt, her ears and cheeks sometimes turn bright red. But today, I don't know—maybe sallow is the right word, the way your skin might get if you lived in the depths of the forest and never saw daylight.

But she's doing well. The doctor said so. The nurse I told to go fuck herself said so. Even the obtuse Miss Tania said so. Probably I'm just imagining the fluorescent sheen to her skin that catches my eye once in a while.

Nadia and Spring are dancing wildly around the living room to old Grateful Dead tunes, something of a ritual in our house whenever Nadia manages to extricate herself early from the damp grip of her boss at *Ulster Today*.

The magazine, which has very little reason to exist, has gone through four editors in the three years Nadia has been working there. This one—they all seem to be named Mike or Bob—is fresh out of grad school, wears cowboy boots, and drinks beer in the office. But they all seem to expect Nadia to work late, and to give up all other aspects of her life for the greater glory of photographic essays about the Rondout Creek.

For this is all a dream we dreamed one afternoon long ago! Spring is bellowing. Nadia has her up in the air, whirling around, jumping up on the black leather couch. I'm exhausted just watching them. But I like watching them. It's one of the few things I really do like. It suggests that life is actually being lived here and not merely somewhere else.

"Come on, Daddy!" She's reaching her skinny little arms out to me to join the dance, so I do. I lope into their little circle and flap my arms like an awkward crane. Although I never think of myself as tall, when I stand next to Spring (tiny) and Nadia (petite), I tower over them and my long arms cast little shadows on their heads in the late afternoon light.

The phone rings. I let Nadia answer it.

After the incident, we got a lot of calls—hospital staff, lawyers, even a reporter from the *Kingston Freeman*, who claimed to be doing an article on childhood head trauma. I figured he was just poking around in the detritus of our fragile lives, and I told him to go fuck himself, something I find myself saying over the phone far more often than is wise. This may be why Nadia does not mind that I don't answer the phone much anymore.

"Is it Pop-Pop?" Spring demands. I intuit from the way Nadia scrunches up her amazing eyes that it is indeed her father, running late as usual on his Northampton-to-Phoenicia journey.

She hands off the phone to Spring, who immediately begins singing into the phone, *"Just a box of rain, I don't know who put it there."* I think I hear Dr. Maire's sonorous voice over the phone, joining her in song, which is really almost too much to bear.

In the kitchen, Nadia furiously chops up carrots. "He's such a jerk sometimes," she mutters.

"Your dad *is* a jerk, but Spring loves him."

Nadia giggles. She has a high-pitched child's voice—the only thing childish about her; sometimes she and Spring sound so alike I'm not sure who is speaking. "Not my dad. I mean, he is a jerk too, I guess, but I was talking about Mike the boy editor. Oh, I'm sick of bad boys."

"Does that mean you're sick of me?"

"You're not bad. Impossible, maybe. This guy wanted me to redo a whole shoot on 'The Bars of New Paltz' because there weren't enough pictures of *chicks with tattoos*. He actually used those words. I told him I had to head home, my old sick father was coming for a visit." She laughs. When she laughs, she tends to throw her whole head back, like she can't control it. "Dad would love to hear that, I'm sure."

"He wouldn't hear it, probably."

"Not if I said it, anyway." She drifts over to me, puts her slender arms around me. "He much prefers you to me, you know; I think he only decided to re-Dad himself when he realized I had married someone almost as weird as he is."

She kisses me—an afterthought, but a pleasant one.

Spring bounces in. "Hungry! Ooohh, Mommy and Daddy kissing! Yay!"

I lift her up, fling her onto my shoulder.

"How come some mommies and daddies kiss and some don't? How come some kids have two mommies and some have two daddies and some have only one and some don't have any at all? Can I marry you, Daddy? How come Pop-Pop has been married so many times? Can a dog marry a cat? Can a dog marry a necklace?"

I shake my head at the wide range of her five-year-old, cannot-be-answered questions.

Nadia takes her, smoothes her hair. "What did Pop-Pop say on the phone?"

"He'll be here soon, soon, soon. Told him about the horsies at my school. Told him Agnes wants to meet him."

Nadia carries her to the sink. "Almost dinner. Wash your hands. One of the horses wants to meet Pop-Pop?"

"No, silly, my friend. The green girl."

Nadia looks at me. I think I must have coughed, coughed really loudly, that's the kind of look I'm getting. She wants to say something, I can see that, but she doesn't, just methodically takes out paper napkins, forks, and knives, hands them to Spring, who loves to help set the table.

"Milk or apple juice?"

"Milky, milky!"

"So this girl Agnes? Does she...wear green clothes all the time?"

"Sometimes."

"Does she really look green?"

"Sort of green."

"Do other kids see her?"

"I don't know. Daddy sees her."

I roll my eyes, catch a sharp look from Nadia. I walk briskly to the stove, take out the roast chicken, poke at it, poke at it very thoroughly, more thoroughly than any chicken has ever been poked. "Should we wait for your father? This bird is definitely ready."

Spring skips into the dining room, bounds into her booster seat, singing, *Just a box of rain, I don't know who put it there...*

I smile my little forced smile. I start to carve. Nadia comes up behind me. "Is she okay?" she whispers. "Is she hallucinating? Some weird lingering thing from the hematoma?"

"She's okay, she's okay," I say, and I am pleased to hear myself say it so emphatically, so reassuringly. "She's singing,"

I continue, only now my words sound too loud, too fast. "She's okay okay okay...Dr. Balin said so...active eating happy...SHE IS OKAY!"

"Great," Nadia says. "Are you?"

14.

"Of course I know Grunwald!" Dr. Maire shouts, gesturing toward our chandelier with a forkful of roast chicken. His hands, I have often noticed, seem to operate independently from the rest of his body.

"We met years ago. Millbrook? I think so, though it might have been Esalen. I even lectured at the Grunwald Center back in the eighties. On the lore of the changeling, the child stolen away by Others, replaced by the shriveled creature who fails to thrive—how those tales resonate with our modern horror of the autistic child. And back in the day, I donated something to the Center. Now what was it? Something meaningful, though now I cannot recall what. Well, that was before we had our little falling-out—a disagreement, let us say, on Grunwald's controversial treatment. Funny, though, is it not, Paul? That you should end up living so near his little lair? That this Jack should pull you into Grunwald's orbit on the very day that I show up? Dr. Jung might call it synchronous, don't you think so?"

"I hope not."

———

Spring is sitting on a folding chair next to him with her head in his lap; I think she has fallen asleep but I can't see her eyes, which are covered by the forward flop of her hair. In between bites of cold chicken (he was two hours late) and sautéed green beans, punctuated by his usual exclamatory arm-waving, Dr. Maire strokes her forehead with one finger, a sweet gesture which almost makes me forgive the rest of his shtick.

"Look at her, little sleeping elf," he murmurs. "Such a wondrous age—everything magic to them. If only we grown-ups could keep that consciousness, hmmm?"

"You've managed, haven't you, Dad?" Nadia says. She is cleaning the counter, which she already cleaned before, somewhat furiously swabbing the table where I am still sitting. "You didn't tell me Jack was here today."

"Sorry...didn't...didn't have time. Something's wrong with the twins. That's what Jack says, anyway. I think you'll be seeing your beloved cousin Gwen soon."

"Did Jack mention whether she still has that stick up her butt?" She scoops Spring from Dr. Maire's lap. "Way past bedtime for you, little widget." She passes her around for sleepy kisses, then off to the bathroom.

"Night, Pop-Pop," Spring whispers. "You staying here tonight? Take me to school tomorrow, okay?"

He deftly kisses the top of her head but does not commit to this radical course of action. For a few moments, there is only his munching and the faint sound of Chopin etudes coming from the living room. I find myself staring at the dining room table, as if fascinated by the swirls of the pine.

"So, Paul," he says finally, wiping the chicken grease from his mouth, "you have something to ask me, I think."

I look up—startled, I guess, because he laughs. He has a tight, dry chuckle, nothing like Nadia's gorgeous guffaw.

"No, I have not become psychic in my old age…not more than previously, anyway. But I am a terribly good observer of body language and I do notice…well, for one thing, you haven't left the room, which you usually do if you and I are alone. Did you know this?"

"Umm…no," I murmur, looking down again.

"And look at you, leaning in toward the table, in my direction, head held down almost as if it were being thrust there. This is a clear sign, it seems to me, that you wish to look up, to look at me, to engage me, to ask me…what?"

What?

What indeed?

I get up from the chair, pace around the room. I look out each window at the soft darkness of early June evening as a few cars whiz down High Street and a trio of deer grazes on the edge of the field across the road. One looks up, gazing at me with strangely reddish eyes. I shudder.

I start to tell him. I tell about my lost-in-the-forest dreams, not in detail, not with any great emotion, just the bare bones, just the words carefully, quietly. And then I tell him about the girl, the green girl I have seen first in my dream and then darting around our yard and the school. I don't tell him that Spring sees her too. I don't tell him how terrified I feel sometimes when I see this girl, as if she were a portent of something darker yet to come. I don't even mention that sometimes when I look at Spring I catch a faint aura of green. I just tell him that she's like an apparition only not, that she seems more real than that. That she seems to have sprung right from the center of Dadd's painting.

He rubs his chin. He drums two fingers on his cheekbone. He wags one finger at the ceiling, nods slightly.

I stop speaking, but I haven't said—can't say—all that there is to say. "The thing is," I stammer, "I never…I never had

dreams like this until Spring...until the incident. I never saw
green girls, never...I've seen other things sometimes, things
that I wasn't sure were there, but never like this because she
seems like she is there, like she's part of a story. My story."

I sit down, fold my hands like a good little schoolboy.

"A story, yes," he says. "It is a story, you are right, Paul. Have
you ever heard of the Green Children of Woolpit?"

I shake my head, though he is not looking at me.

"In the thirteenth century, I believe, two children, green as
peas, were found wandering through the town of Woolpit, Suf-
folk. Spoke no English, could not tell anyone where they were
from, would eat no food except raw beans. Some in the village
said they had dreamed of them. Some said they were faery folk,
some said demons, some said changelings—children stolen by
the little men and given back green and empty like husks. The
boy died, the girl lived. Eventually, the story goes, she learned
English, told everyone she was from a land under the ground—
St Martin's Land, she called it. She told everyone that she and
her brother had seen a green light shining in a cave, followed it
to the town, and could not find their way back to St. Martin's
Land. Swore that there was a world inside this world, one most
can't see. She grew older and forgot everything about her world,
married some village boy, melted away into the great nothing-
ness of the world. One of those anomalous events no one can
explain. Fascinating, yes?"

"But...a legend, right? Some bullshit medieval legend...?"

"Ah, but there have been other sightings of green children
in more recent years. In Spain, in Kyrgyzstan, in Nova Scotia.
In dreams, in horrifying night terrors. Fascinating, I think, that
green, so beloved now in our culture, considered so benign—
lovely sweet nature!—is perceived in these tales as ominous.
Like in your dream, Paul. Something dark and outside understanding, some part of the collective unconscious perhaps not

fully grasped by our day-to-day minds. Once I planned to write a book about that but I didn't, I can't recall why."

And I couldn't recall why I thought he might be able to help me, either. "But what do you think it means, that I see this girl? That I dream this girl and then see her? Is it...is she... some kind of warning to me? About Spring? Am I dreaming this because of Spring's...incident? Because I couldn't...almost didn't...save her? Am I dreaming the green girl into life? Am I dreaming when I see her...outside...in the world?"

"Are you dreaming this conversation?" he replied. "Cannot help you there. Warning? My friend Fritz Perls once said that a dream is a letter sent from one part of consciousness to another. Perhaps this is a letter that needs to be sent over and over, and perhaps it has tumbled out of your dream life into what we like to call the real world, hmmm? That swinging door effect we spoke of once, as if some voice from the Secret Inside of the World were speaking to you, through you. It could be, could be."

"What could be?" Nadia asks, gently closing the door to Spring's tiny room.

I jerk my head toward her, vaguely guilty. She smiles her gorgeous smile, as if it were an unalloyed pleasure to see her husband and her father deep in conversation. I smile back, sheepishly, knowing what little comfort she would take in the off-kilter image of the world just offered up in this room, in words which seem to hang there like a puff of foul-smelling smoke.

Dr. Maire stretches, yawns. This is his métier, after all, and nothing new. "What indeed?" he asks. "What indeed? Now where am I sleeping tonight?"

15.

Dr. Maire lies on our black leather couch in a quite indecorous pose, his long bare legs jutting out of the lime-green sheets, his arms crossed over his head. His snoring and mumbling are almost as loud as the dull hum of The Discovery Channel, which plays continuously in the background whenever he visits.

Something about mass delusion is on, which I'm sure he would enjoy, except he's dead asleep, as are all members of the household except me.

I can't sleep, can never sleep, often wake five or six times, hearing faint squeaks in a corner of the room. Nadia likes to joke that a bird chirping in the next county wakes me up, though to me this isn't so farfetched.

All my life I've been this way. Exhausted, I sometimes pass out on the couch or the chair, but whenever I lurch awake and go to bed, sleep eludes me. I must sleep sometimes—I know that I dream, I dream vividly—but when I finally come back to consciousness, I usually feel as if the night has passed over me completely, leaving me sore and restless.

Sex doesn't make me sleepy, alcohol doesn't make me sleepy, even the pounds of opiated black hashish my dead friend Tommy used to import from Morocco could not do the job. Everyone else in our dorm would be slumped over and I'd still be sitting up, eyes wide with things that might or might not be there.

Nadia tried to help me sleep tonight. That was her rationale, anyway, though I think she just likes having sex when her father is in the next room, hoping to make him uncomfortable. Not that anything makes the man uncomfortable, as far as I can tell.

After he yawned loudly and announced he was kicking us out of our own living room, Nadia nudged me into our bedroom, sat me down on the bed, and tried to get me to tell her what we'd been discussing. I told her dreams, just dreams, and she immediately got that look in her eyes, the *I'm so over the unconscious* look she gets whenever I stray into what she perceives as her father's realm. Then she pulled off her blouse, her jeans. "Bet I can give you some sweet dreams."

I wasn't going to say no.

She looks great, her body barely showing the stretch marks, the scars of Spring's birth. Okay, she's only twenty-six, has plenty of reasons to look great. And her skin is a truly fine shade of off-white, and I was all ready to fling myself onto her, but she held out her hand. "Nope, my treat," she whispered.

She pushed me back onto the bed as if we were still in our courting phase—not that there was much courting. She was in flight from a crazy ex and basically moved into my tiny Upper West Side apartment a few days after we had our first date.

"Tonight, you're my prisoner," she promised, and so I was.

We don't do this much anymore. Not much of anything anymore. One or the other of us is usually too tired or too agitated, or Spring is awake, or Nadia is dashing off to work, or I'm trying to shake off/avoid bad dreams.

Sometimes I worry that Nadia—far better looking and younger than anyone I deserve—might be tempted by one of the bad Bobs or Mikes in her office. But then she'll whisper something sweet or exciting in my ear, stroke my face, tell me that I make her feel beautiful, make her feel sexy. These are things she whispers to me sometimes, and who doesn't like to hear that?

"You were so quiet," she said, leaping up. "Not sexy enough for you?" She jumped back onto the bed, cupped her hands over her mouth in a mock shout. "Or is it that Dad is just a wall away?" She laughed, pulled on her long white nightshirt, flopped onto the pillows.

I was still lying there as if pinioned to our sweaty sheets, trying to keep the moment alive, trying not to let my thoughts race toward what they usually race toward.

She lifted her beautiful head. "You don't think there's something wrong with Spring like Jack thinks there's something wrong with his boys? That she sees things? That she sees things that aren't there?"

"She's five. Your father says that's the magical age, the age when they can't really tell the difference between what's real and what isn't..."

"Can you?" She looked grave suddenly. "Maybe you should call the doctor tomorrow."

"About her or about me?"

"I'm worried about you, but I'm used to your moods and your weird ideas. But Spring...what if there's still bleeding or something and they didn't get it out or it wasn't just a fall, it was something else. You know, a seizure? So please call him, just make sure."

"He's such an asshole."

"So is my father, but you just quoted him to me. Call Dr. Balin tomorrow, okay? See what he says about this green girl?"

I started to cite objections, but she had already fallen asleep, so I pulled on my clothes and tiptoed into the living room.

Now I stare at Dr. Maire's sleeping form, puzzling over what he said about the Green Children, whether it makes any sense, whether I have any reason whatsoever to pay attention to his almost jazz-like riffs on the paranormal.

Out on Woodland Valley Road, a lone truck chugs up the hill, and a large dark figure, maybe a bear or a big black dog, ambles along Herdman Road Bridge. I have sat like this before. I have sat like this and cried before and that's what I'm doing now because all I can think of—even though I know she's okay, I know she's okay—all I can think of is the night of the incident.

We arrived home from London at two AM, the long drive from Kennedy punctuated by Nadia and Spring breathing quietly, curled up in the back seat while I drove us home. We left the suitcases piled up in the hallway, and I didn't even check our answering machine or lock the door. I could barely see straight. Nadia whisked our jetlagged child into bed. But she wouldn't sleep. She cried and tossed, and Nadia finally got her, brought her into bed with us, wrapped her in her arms, shushed her, cooed to her, and I must have fallen asleep because when I jolted awake, she was not in bed next to me, was not in Nadia's arms, was nowhere to be seen.

I stumbled out of the bedroom. The front door was cracked open, and when I rushed to the door I saw Spring clambering up the wooden swing set in the side yard, one of her little arms outstretched, as if trying to touch someone's hand.

"Spring!" I yelled, "Jesus! Get down!"

And just as I said it, she made a funny noise, a high-pitched laugh—a swooning sound, almost. And then she crumpled, pitching off the very top of the swing set, hitting the ground headfirst before I could get there.

The rest is a blur. She sat up immediately, said she was fine, wondered where she was, wondered why she was outside in the middle of the night. She seemed okay. Amazingly, there was no blood. Not a scratch. I carried her back to bed, but the next morning she couldn't wake up, seemed dull and listless, her eyes vacant, like she was not there. She threw up. Nadia was terrified, and when Spring threw up three more times, she called our (former) pediatrician who said, *She's fine. A stomach virus, probably. Just watch her,* and we did, and Nadia even went to work but a few hours later, I couldn't stop thinking how bad Spring looked, skin sort of greenish, eyes empty, not laughing, not eating, not speaking. Almost gone. I grabbed her, struggled with the car seat but finally strapped her in, then drove like a madman down Route 28 to Benedictine Hospital. I called Nadia, kept calling and calling her and couldn't reach her, and the doctors looked at Spring and said, *Oh my God, another hour and she would have been dead, we have to do an emergency craniotomy. There's blood throughout the cranium. You should have brought her sooner!* And I cried and wanted to die.

Nadia finally arrived and we both cried and we went into the tiny chapel in the hospital and Nadia, whose mother was a good Catholic, knelt and prayed, and I slumped into the red velvet pew and whispered *Please, please, let me be the one to go, not her. Please don't take her, please don't take her...*

But the operation was a complete success, and she survived, and then the circus began. The doctors were certain she could not have simply fallen. She must have had a seizure or been flung to the ground. There must have been more to this than a horrible accident. There must be abuse, must be reckless endangerment, and a parade of officials made us repeat the story over and over. *Tell us about the incident,* they said. It was always *the incident,* never *the accident. Why was she outside at night?* they wondered. *Was she running from you? Has she ever had a seizure? Have you ever blacked out?*

They asked Nadia, *Do you ever feel jealous of the attention she gets from your husband?* They demanded from me, *Do you ever feel that having a child has ruined your lifestyle?*

Are you a normal human being? Or are you a monster?

For almost a week, they kept Spring in that crappy little hospital under observation, and Nadia stayed with her, camping out on the foldout couch in her room. Every night I would drive back up the hill, sit in front of this same window and cry. I would not answer the phone. I did not tell a soul what had happened.

The nurses in the head trauma unit kept at Nadia. *Was it a seizure? Is your husband neglectful?* One of them made Nadia cry—and very little makes my resilient wife cry—and I told them they would hear from our lawyer (though we have no lawyer), and finally they backed off, postponed any further harassment until the worst week of our lives had passed, and Spring, miraculously recovered, could go home.

Then they started calling again, saying they needed to see where the incident occurred. Nadia, furious, went to *Ulster Magazine*'s lawyer, who shrugged as if we were making much of nothing. "Just allow them to see your house," he sighed. "They'll let it go."

But when we finally agreed someone could come to the house to check out the "scene" of the incident, they told us they did not believe they would see what they needed to see. "You will have fixed things up," the nurse said. "It's meaningless now. But we will be keeping an eye on you."

Which is when I told her to go fuck herself, and she said, very calmly to me, "There is an old saying, Mr. Brickner. *The trouble is not now, the trouble is yet to come.*"

I guess I must have muttered that last sentence out loud just now, because Dr. Maire is suddenly sitting up, his wispy hair plastered onto his forehead. "That is so true, Paul," he rasps. "Trouble. Yet to come."

He lowers himself back onto the couch, rolls over, and falls into a deep, pitiless sleep.

16.

Dakota the doula never did approve of me.

"What does a doula do, anyway?" I asked her the first time we met. A natural question, I thought, though I could have gone years without caring about the answer.

Nadia, Dakota, and I were sitting in our cramped living room on W. 83rd Street, trying not to knock over wine glasses as we shifted uncomfortably on the dwarf couch. Dakota's shoulders are as broad as my own; she is what my mother would have called big-boned.

"A doula does what men don't do," she snapped, removing her knee from its tenuous spot against mine.

"Shop?" I asked.

"Help." She practically spat the word at me. That may be how I first sensed her lack of approval.

She was not around the year that Nadia met me, bonded with me, moved into that apartment and reordered my wildly askew life. She was in Paris, some Wesleyan study abroad program. When she returned, she was dismayed to discover that Nadia had ditched Fred, her crazy ex, and had taken up with me.

Not that she approved of Fred either. In fact, she once told Nadia she planned to organize an intervention, urging all of their college friends to gather and denounce Fred for being abusive. Nadia laughed at her. "Fred can't even swat mosquitoes," she pointed out.

I also have it from a reliable source (okay, Nadia) that Dakota can't stand Dr. Maire either, so maybe it's all the men in Nadia's life she finds wanting. Or men in general, I'm not sure—though she was at pains that first day to elaborate on why she became a doula, whatever that is. I still don't really know.

"Only women know how to help women," she said. "Men just screw it up."

It's not so much that I disagree with that observation, I would just prefer not to have the heavy hand of her contempt resting so squarely on my head.

Like Pearl, Dakota was convinced I'd be a bad dad. But now, today, she tells me she realizes I'm not a bad dad, not a bad dad at all. She even seems to like me a little. And that's good, because unlike most of Nadia's friends (the rageful Jennifer, the wraith-like Lauren), Nadia takes what Dakota says seriously.

"You're devoted to that little sweetie, aren't you?" she noted with mild wonderment this afternoon as I was pacing the hallway, waiting to see if Dr. Maire actually remembered to pick up his grandchild from preschool. "So maybe I misjudged you, Paul." She punched me in the arm, smiled at me for the first time ever.

During the wedding, Dakota was definitely part of the glower committee. She declined to look at me during the ceremony, but I wasn't bothered because I felt the same way myself. Who would want to look at me when they could look at Nadia, her reddish-black hair piled high on her exquisite head, a sight to see, even if she was visibly pregnant and had thrown up a few minutes before her grand entrance.

At the dinner afterward, Dakota and Pearl scrunched up against Nadia at the banquet table and glared at me like two-thirds of a see-no-evil, hear-no-evil, speak-no-evil tableau. And then there was the dance.

Most of the weddings I've attended featured muddy guitars and bass competing with braying balladeers. Or raucous disco and novelty numbers—horrifying chicken dances, ethnic frolicking of all kinds. I said I didn't want that kind of crap at our wedding, and neither did Nadia. I would have loved to have Tommy play, but he was dead—and in truth, he didn't cover himself with glory at my second wedding when he was alive (more or less). He literally nodded out, strumming his guitar while slurring the chorus to "Will the Circle Be Unbroken."

So, we agreed: no mortifyingly inappropriate wedding band. Instead, Nadia asked Pearl to find us a DJ to spin some tunes we actually might like to hear at our happy event. Why on earth did she think her mother was capable of finding such a person? Well, to be fair she was distracted, still suffering from morning sickness and consumed with finding a dress in which she wouldn't feel fat.

She was also wrestling with who would perform the unlikely ceremony (her mother's second cousin, as it turned out, a minister from some anonymous Protestant sect), and whether she should include Dr. Maire in the festivities. She left it to her mother to arrange for the food (good) and the music (bad). So what we got was Long John DiSantis, a local Connecticut radio personality. "I will fill your special night with songs!" he bellowed to Nadia in the one telephone conversation we had with him.

Our non-negotiable demands: no Billy Joel, no Elton John, no BeeGees, no disco of any kind. Our first song was to be Elvis's "I Can't Help Falling In Love With You," because Nadia swoons for Elvis despite the fact he died decades ago.

But when the time came, Long John (who looked alarmingly like Ichabod Crane) couldn't seem to find that song, and instead played Billy Joel's "Honesty," arguably the worst song ever written. It devolved from there. He kept making announcements like, "Okay, friends and family of the happy couple, let's see the in-laws dance!" Except there weren't any in-laws present (my father was dead, my mother in Florida, my sister too wrapped up in suburban angst). And then there was, "Okay, the groom dances with the maid of honor and the bride with the best man, let's go!"

I didn't really have an official best man, but Jack was there and swirled off with Nadia while his wife Gwen joined in the glower fest. Dakota stood before me, head cocked, a little smirk playing about her lips, as if to say, "What are you going to do now, Paul?"

What could I do? I put a tentative arm around her big waist and made as if to dance. But the song old Long John spun for us was Lennon's "I Want You So Bad." I defy anyone to dance to that tune.

I tried. Sort of. We must have resembled a couple suddenly struck by a neurological disorder, twitching and stumbling in awkward circles, until Dakota, looking upward as if to heaven, burst into giggles and I shrugged and walked away.

I didn't see her again until the night the baby was born, when she pretty much elbowed me out of the way in the delivery room. "You'll just mess it up," Dakota declared. "I don't care how many Lamaze classes you sat through."

Which was fine with me. My father's generation had the right idea about childbirth: the man sits out in the waiting room, smoking a pipe and fretting, while the women come and go, and the doctor—also a woman in this case—does the job.

I didn't care much until Spring was there, crimson in the fluorescent glow of the delivery room, with a full head of thick black hair and a perfectly formed smile of a mouth even when she was squalling.

Pearl was there too, reaching out to hold her only grand-child, but Nadia said, "No! Let her daddy have her first!" So Dakota reluctantly handed the baby to me.

I trembled, afraid that the slippery eel of an infant would wriggle right out of my hands. Instead she stopped crying, looked up at me with half-closed eyes, and sighed. And I was a goner. I still am.

"Aunt Dakota is here! Hurray!" Spring shouts as she runs up the steps, through the door, and leaps into Dakota the doula's ample arms. Dr. Maire is still trudging up the driveway. He's carrying Spring's backpack in one hand and clutching a large branch of lavender in the other. He looks puzzled, too, some-thing I rarely see on his self-satisfied face.

"These are for you," he says, shooting me a strange look. "Some feral child at Spring's school insisted I give them to you. Her friend Agnes? Strange little girl. Looks unwell, wouldn't you say?"

Dakota whirls by, lifting the giggling Spring above her head. I intercept my girl, bring her back down to earth. "What's Pop-Pop talking about?" I ask. "Did you and your green friend play today?"

Dakota stops whirling. She narrows her eyes at me. "Did you call that doctor today?" she asks.

I feel a rush of heat to my forehead. "Are you here to spy on me? Did Nadia ask you to come and spy on me?"

She smiles, but it's more of a wince. "Not at all," she says, unconvincingly. "We talked, is all."

"Agnes wasn't there today," Spring says, looking from me to Dakota and back. "Or maybe she was, but she wasn't let-

ting me see her." She runs off toward the refrigerator. "Milk!
Milk!"

I place the lavender branch on the table and all the petals
immediately fall off. The branch looks withered in its naked-
ness, and Dr. Maire stares at it, shrugging to himself, as if at a
puzzle that, for once, he cannot quite assemble.

17.

Back before Tommy was dead, he used to lurch across the world in an unlikely orange Volvo station wagon. He bought it at a police auction after his father died and left him far less money than he had been anticipating.

"This fucker is all that's left of my WASP legacy," he declared. "So just like my life, I'm going to run it into the ground!" And he did, screeching around corners, barreling down dark highways, rarely bothering to look in either the real or the metaphorical rearview mirror.

Once, when I was still living in Connecticut, he showed up, insisting I drive with him to the Auberon, some old resort hotel turned into a nightclub near Litchfield, where the junkie diva Nico was playing. He knew Nico from Amsterdam. They had performed together in some glorified opium den there, and he had it in mind that he could play at the Auberon too—just show up, accompany Nico on guitar, and restart his largely imaginary music career.

Laura, my first wife, was still around (she wasn't around long), and I can still see her cowering in the back seat as Tommy drove a hundred miles an hour through the twisting back roads of northwestern Connecticut.

He had taken mescaline or something, and he was talking very fast about the lush, green summer evening, the beautiful trees and vines and bushes all around us, blooming everywhere—*reaching out their little hands,* I remember him saying, *their little leafy hands*—and suddenly, without actually stopping the car, he slowed a little and opened the door, shouting, "I can't take this anymore!" and rolled out of the car as it hurtled down the road.

"Jesus!" I said, and grabbed the wheel, somehow managing to stop us on the side of Route 202. Tommy was just lying in a ditch like a beached whale, utterly unhurt, laughing, laughing.

So, now, driving my own only slightly less unlikely station wagon, heading to Dr. Balin's office with Dakota strapped in the back seat next to Spring, I find myself thinking of that moment, wishing I could be as grandly irresponsible as Tommy, ditch the car and shout, "I just can't take this," and roll away.

I'm sure that's what Dakota thinks I might do anyway. She keeps checking on me, peering into the front seat she so conspicuously declined to sit in, as if I might slam the dashboard with my fist—sure, I've been thinking about it—and veer off the road, all because I got a little peevish when I grasped that she was not here on a spontaneous visit but rather a spy mission, a spy mission set up by my own beloved wife.

"It isn't true!" Dakota blurts out again, without my even mentioning it.

I grit my teeth as we head up Route 28 to the Arkville Wellness Center, where the eccentric Dr. Balin's family practice office hours are being held today.

After Spring's incident, we ditched our pediatrician—a well-regarded local stalwart, whom I would dearly love to have sued and *did* tell to go fuck herself—for the oddball Balin, who splits his time among strangely inappropriate offices all over Ulster and Greene counties.

"Paul, I am not a spy," Dakota exclaims. "I am just a friend; I love your daughter, I love your wife, I'm just along for the, you know, ride."

"Aunt Dakota's a spy! Aunt Dakota's a spy!" Spring chants next to her, elfish eyes glittering with amusement.

"And when will you be filing your report?" I ask as we pull into the muddy driveway.

"This is it?" she asks. "It looks more like a Quonset hut than a doctor's office."

I shrug. "Sorry. We're not in Larchmont. Maybe you should jot that down for further discussion."

I open the back door to unsnap Spring, but Dakota has already gotten her out of the car seat, lifting her up with her big hands. I start up the stairs but Spring whimpers, "Daddy, I don't want to go, I don't like Dr. Balin."

"Nobody does, sweetie." I take her hand and race up the steps with her, as if I could simply leave Dakota standing in the driveway. But she's right behind us, striding purposefully toward our appointment.

We sit in the colorless lobby, glancing at ancient magazines. Spring plays with a box of Legos. I lean over toward Dakota. "So tell me again…why are you here?"

"Okay, Paul. I get it. You don't like being doubted. Nadia is my friend, though. She wanted a healthcare professional's opinion on how Spring is doing. That's all."

"You are not actually a doctor, though, are you? Or a nurse? Or a medical technician? Or even a midwife? So what is it that she thinks you might notice about Spring's health that I'm not noticing?"

"Spring Maire-Brickner?" the receptionist blares. "Right this way, little one." She takes Spring's tiny hand and I follow and Dakota follows me, as if she were some sort of family member, which, as I point out, she isn't.

"I will not say a word, Paul. I just want to check this doctor out, okay?"

I feel like phoning Nadia right now and lodging a complaint. But I don't. I beam at the expressionless Dr. Balin, a family practice physician who seems to have no real attachment to families, and say, "What's up, Doc?" in my best moron's voice, and Spring giggles.

He looks in eyes, checks back of head, feels glands, listens to heart, listens to lungs, says nothing.

"Her mother wonders…" Dakota starts. She looks at me, then hesitates.

"You're not the mother?" Dr. Balin asks, though he's met Nadia several times.

"Her mother worries that she's not one hundred percent," I say, finally, and sigh. I don't mean for the sigh to escape, it just does. "The accident. The fall. She's been saying some things that her mother thinks might be…she's worried there might be…"

"Neurological damage?" Dakota jumps in.

"Why?" Dr. Balin asks. "Is she sleepy? Dopey?"

"No, and not sneezy or grumpy either," I add. Spring giggles. No one else does. "Lots of energy, runs around, eats fine. Sees things, her mother worries. Things that aren't there."

"She's five," the doctor observes. "Spring, honey," he finally says, voice sweeter than I would have thought possible, "why is your mommy worried about you? Do you know?"

"She thinks I'm too much like my daddy," she says brightly. I laugh, but the sound sticks in my throat.

"The wound is healing fine," the doctor says, stroking the back of her head. "You can stop giving her the antibiotics."

"See, Daddy, just like Agnes said!"

"She has a…she sees this girl, Agnes…who's green…"

"Kids. Magic." He shrugs, as if I am genuinely dense.

"Daddy sees her sometimes too," Spring burbles. "And Pop-Pop saw her at school today. She gave him a flower."

"You don't think she could be seizure-prone?" Dakota breaks in. "You don't think she could be having migrainous hallucinatory aura?"

Dr. Balin gives her quite a look. Suddenly, I like this guy; suddenly he is one of the best doctors I've ever seen. "If she falls down again, or acts in an unusual way, bring her back. Unusual, that is, not usual for a five-year-old, for a bright and imaginative child who's had a terrible accident but who otherwise seems fine, better than the adults in her life, possibly. How did that Zoloft work out for you, by the way?"

"It didn't."

He throws up his hands. I know the feeling, but Spring leaps down from the table, shouting, "Yay! I'm okay!" She races out of the examining room and down the hall.

Dakota sits there, slumped in the too-small chair as if all the air had seeped out of her. "Doc," I say, as he turns to leave, "do you know this Child Retrieval Center? This Dr. Grunwald?"

He stops. "Why?"

"Just wondering," I say. "Local educational resource and all."

He strokes his chin and nibbles his lower lip. "Trouble," he says, then strides into another office, slams the door.

18.

So, I left Nadia.

Okay, I only left her for a few hours, but it feels good to say it. Empowering, Dakota might call it, though that word makes me think of some noisy machine, a motorcycle revving its engine loudly in my head.

But, yes, I was aggrieved and angry—and I try not to get angry, it rarely goes well for me—to be mistrusted by the only woman who ever really believed in me.

Did I imagine this? Imagine her belief in me? It lifted me up, armed me in some way. Sort of the way, in Peter Pan, you're asked to clap if you believe in fairies and you do and thus Tinkerbell is saved, her little light not snuffed out. That's how I think about Nadia. How because of her my little light was not snuffed out.

Once, during the snuffed-out phase of my second marriage, Annie fixed me with her blue eyes and said, "Congratulations, Paul, you win the passive-aggressive spouse of the year award."

"What does that even mean?" I managed. I had not said any more words to her than that in days.

"You're gone, but you won't leave," she said. We were face to face in our sunless living room for the first time all week. "It would be so much better if it were the other way around."

But with Nadia, I never wanted to leave. Even today I just wanted to slam a door, stomp, make a point. So I did. She and Dakota and Spring were dancing around the kitchen, making sugar cookies in the shape of forest creatures. And I could have joined them. Instead, I kicked a chair and headed out the door to join Dr. Maire, who suddenly had the notion to drive up Pantherkill Road and see his former friend and colleague, jolly Dr. Grunwald.

I must have made my point—some point, anyway—because Nadia came rushing out of the kitchen, flour all over her black silk blouse. She hugged me in the doorway.

"You're going with my father?" she asked me, eyes scrunched up in mock horror. "You hate me, don't you?"

"I hate being spied on."

She handed me a slightly burned cookie that vaguely resembled a deer. "It was a lame idea. It was. I was worried, that's all. It's not like you're so forthcoming, so emotionally available since the accident. I don't always know what to think."

"Me neither," I said, and I walked out the door.

But I looked back—I always look back. I would so have been turned into a pillar of salt in ancient days—and Nadia was still standing there, small in the big doorway, arms outstretched for a moment, and then I was on the cement steps, following her father, who is no one I ever imagined following.

"Well, Paul," he says, squinting at the steep hill of Woodland Valley Road, "let's take a little journey, shall we?"

"I thought we were checking out Grunwald's lair."

"And so we are," he declares, jauntily waving an arm out the window. "But look at this day. Glorious. Must we go directly there? No. Should we not take a spin? We should."

We screech up the road, take a turn I've never even noticed, a little bridge heading left into the valley.

"Where are we going, then?"

"*Go Round About, Peer Gynt,* the Great Boyg says. Do you know that play, Paul? Ibsen's trolls and hill folk, I have always thought, are very close to Dadd's greenish creatures. Frightening, perhaps, because they are so like us, sunk in desire and deceit."

I am trying not to get annoyed. I am trying not to notice how long this little roundabout is taking, and how odd it is that the Woodland Valley Creek seems to be on both sides of the road here. On the shadowed side an old man hunched over a canvas paints the brackish landscape. I am very tempted to leap out of the car and join him.

Houses, many of them boarded up, loom above the road. I hear the howling of dogs chained up in the yard and children shrieking through a field.

"Shouldn't we be heading in the other direction?" I ask, trying with no success to mask my impatience.

"Where? Chez Grunwald? We will be there. In good time. Going roundabout."

Down by the creek, several rubber-clad fishermen, looking like something out of a Brueghel painting, silently throw their lines into the water and reel them in, over and over.

"Your friend Jack's boys—what do you know about them?" He cranes toward me as if only now becoming aware of my presence. "Does he fear they are on the spectrum?"

"I don't know what he fears." I know what I fear. I fear I will be caught up in one of Dr. Maire's rambling discourses.

"Autism? Is that what he trembles about? What so many parents tremble about these days? You know, Grunwald believes what the ancients believed: that these children, call them autistic if you must, these not-quite-there children, are changelings. Not taken away by faery folk, no, but split in two, their consciousness divided, even as young as two or three, yes, split into shadow and self. The dark side of their little burgeoning personae overtaking them. Rid them of the shadow, he thinks, and they will be whole. But how? How does he do that? Isolation. Aversion therapy. A great pressing down onto them of the weight of selfhood, a driving out of the Other, a closing up of the bag into which all their dark impulses have been placed."

He pounds the steering wheel as if it were a lectern.

"But I do not see it the same way. Not at all. There is trouble there. Trouble yet to come. For how does he diagnose these changelings? That is significant! A bombardment, if you will, a storm of dark images, horrific pictographs of the twisted soul, images you know very well yourself, Paul. Images meant to seize. To seize their little minds. To immerse them in a frightening world and watch them respond. But is that sound? Is that not somehow the disease itself purporting to be the cure? And are these children not, perhaps, in touch with something important? Some inner truth which we will not or cannot entirely grasp?"

"I have no idea what you're talking about." I sigh. "I really wasn't planning on spending the whole day—"

"Here," he says. "We're here."

I look up, and we are barreling down Pantherkill Road.

"Oh," I say. "I guess we didn't go the usual way."

"No," he beams. "Why would we? You know, there was a Sufi center here back in the day." He glances from side to side, as if he might see something important on the edge of the road. "The adepts would spin and sing *Hu Hu* all day long. I swear you could still hear that sound echoing through the woods, even after Grunwald gutted the place and built his Fortress of Solitude. Are there rabbits hopping across the road or am I imagining it?"

"I don't see anything." He is swerving all over the road, though, as if trying to avoid hitting whatever he sees in his path.

"As I recollect, he called the Sufi center *ghastly*. All that spiritual uplift left over from the Sufi center was bad for the kids, he said. Bad for the patients. Silence is what they need, he told me. Silence and things as they are—concrete, straightforward, no fantasy, no dream. Bring them back from the ether, he called it. Reality not etherality, yes. He said that to me. What ails these troubled children is too much air and not enough earth. Bring them to earth. Press them back down to earth. Yes. Disagreed on this. Earth just as dangerous as ether, I told him. All in how you look at it. What you see."

"I see the parking lot," I tell him.

"We shall go confront Grunwald! We shall intervene in his curious practices!"

The place looks strangely different from yesterday; maybe we are on the other side of the larger-than-necessary parking lot? I didn't notice the maze yesterday, and I definitely didn't notice the guy in green, more like a bouncer than someone in the helping profession. He stands at the top of the maze, his bulging arms crossed, face closed in a scowl.

I like the maze, a leafy zigzag of hedges I know Spring would love to run through. With her friend. Her friend the green girl.

Dr. Maire strides through the bushy twists and turns, deep in his monologue. "Do you recall what I was telling you, Paul, about the Green Children? It is said that they built mazes in every meadow in Woolpit, as if trying, perhaps, to recreate their lost world, the one which lives inside and underneath ours. The girl Agnes, the one who lived, would go out to the hills at night to sleep, even after she was married, they say, arms and legs splayed out as if waiting to sink deep and deeper into it. Into the earth. Perhaps that's what your place needs, Paul: a maze. What do you think? Out by the swing set where you've seen this girl?"

"A…maze…in our yard?" I stammer. "Nadia would have me committed."

But the idea amuses me—more than it should, really—and my laughter sounds odd to my ears, like a shriek almost, like my shriek the night Spring fell. But I stop myself, and Dr. Maire stops too. Not because of me, but because of the goon in green who clamps a big hand on Dr. Maire's bony shoulder.

"Oh, I don't think so," he says.

19.

On the day my father died, I ate magic mushrooms with Tommy and ended up laugh/weeping over a bag of hazelnuts and the memory of an old ax covered in cobwebs in the garage of the house I more or less grew up in.

I didn't know my father would die that day—even Tommy would probably not have recommended we ingest psilocybin as a memento mori. It was a grisly coincidence, the kind that haunted me back then and sometimes still does.

I was twenty-four that day, biding my time at the Columbia School of Journalism and living in a long, dark tunnel of an apartment on W. 112th St. For some reason, Tommy was living in the Berkshires. He had his third or fourth band (this one was called the Amazing Pandas, I think), and they were starting to get gigs in New Wave havens like the Goblin Club in Lenox and Mutation Hall in Williamstown. But he yearned for New York, felt an affinity for its grime and glitter. Periodically, he would appear at my door, bearing gifts.

The day my father died—it was October 1, a day of unearthly early autumn light—Tommy pounded on my door around eight AM. Unsurprisingly, he had been up all night. For several nights, actually. In his hand was a plastic bag of what looked like dirt clods.

He scooped me up in a bear hug. "Paul, Paul, Paul," he crooned. "You will love every minute of these babies. Come away. Come away to the Land of the Lost."

I shrugged. I smiled. I was supposed to be working on a paper about journalistic ethics in the post-Watergate era, for which I felt far less interest than I did for the bag of dirt clods dangling before me.

"Let's sauté them," I suggested. "Then we won't gag."

The kitchen was piled high with dirty dishes and empty pizza boxes—my two roommates were even less prepared for adult life than I was—but I managed to locate olive oil, garlic, a frying pan, and we cooked the mushrooms and ate them on days-old English muffins. I immediately began to feel lightheaded and weird, well before the drug could possibly have kicked in.

For what I think may have been five hours, we sat motionless, frozen on the orange beanbag chairs, the only furniture in that shabby living room. The whole room undulated in the thin light. We listened to scratchy records—the only kind I owned. The Mahavishnu Orchestra, *American Beauty*, Patti Smith— music mostly bequeathed to me by my many and varied ex-girlfriends.

Somehow, some time, we made it out to Central Park, to a fountain where no water was flowing, circled by stone benches littered with fast-food wrappers and cigarette butts. A plastic bag glimmered on the edge of the fountain. It read *Oregon Raw Hazelnuts*, and it had not been opened, just sat there tied with a green plastic twist. Tommy opened the bag.

"I want these!" he bellowed. "I want to eat these!"

"You can't," I pointed out. "They have to be…cracked open. You have to split them in half."

I began to laugh. My eyes streamed with tears. I flashed on the Dadd painting, the man poised to split the hazelnut in half with a golden ax. I grabbed Tommy's arm, tugged at it like he was a recalcitrant pet.

"I've got something to show you," I managed. "We have to go back."

He held onto the bag of hazelnuts and we staggered back to my apartment. Somehow I located the book—*Outsider Art: From Dadd to Darger* by Cheops Liptoffen, one of the few books I had kept from my vast (though largely unread) college collection. I flipped open the dusty pages to the passable reproduction of *The Fairy Feller's Master-Stroke*.

"Look," I said. "A hazelnut."

Tommy immediately fell into a sort of trance, staring at the almost molecular details, the strange meltingness of Dadd's mad vision.

The phone rang.

Even in my twenties the sound of a ringing phone acted like an aversive electric jolt to me. But I picked it up, maybe because it seemed alive, writhing there on the kitchen wall, as if it were in pain.

It was my sister June. She was crying. My sister never called me, and I cannot recall more than two other times that I had ever heard her cry.

"Daddy," she said. "Died this morning. His heart."

I stared at the phone. "When?"

"This morning. Come. Come home."

I hung up.

I stood there. Suddenly, I felt hot, sweaty, burning up. I pulled off my shirt. I walked into the bathroom. I stripped off my clothes, stepped into the moldy shower, turned it on, icy cold, full blast on my head, neck, chest.

I thought about my father. Thinking about him was my only real connection to him. We had not spoken in a year and I could not recall the last time I had touched him. Out of nowhere, I remembered a chilly morning in New Hampshire when I was nine and I woke to a distant *thwock thwock*, a methodical tool sound. It was my father, furiously chopping wood in the back yard. I remembered peering out the window.

Without looking up, my father said, "Paul, come here. I want to show you something."

I shook my head. I had already begun to say no to everything my father asked of me.

"Paul, come here and I will teach you to chop wood," he said.

"No, you won't."

"I will," he said. "If it kills me."

But I would not go out, and he did not teach me, and I never saw him chop wood again and the ax sat in the corner of our garage for the next ten years.

I don't know why that memory flashed before me in the shower, but it did, and it seemed as sad as any story on earth, and I cried.

I found myself dressed, still wet, still crying in the living room while Tommy sat fixated on the Dadd picture.

"He killed his father," I told him.

"Really? I've thought about doing that so many times."

"With an ax. Like that ax. Like my father's ax." And I cried and laughed and gulped and coughed.

"Sometimes," he mused, "I think he's already dead. Then I think, No that's me…"

"My father just died," I said finally.

"What? When?"

"I don't know. Now."

"Now?"

He looked up like he was considering this. Then he pointed to the painting.

"Look at that. That's *now*, isn't it? An eternal now? Like they're all frozen there. Waiting to begin."

"Frozen," I murmured.

And here I am, twenty years and a world away from there, and the painting is still frozen. And so am I, and so are Jack and Gwen, staring up at the damn painting while Dr. Grunwald and my father-in-law are locked in some primal, paralyzing hug. Waiting to begin.

20.

And they all start moving, gesturing, as if someone hit the play button, broke a spell, flipped a switch.

"Paul, old pal," Jack shouts. "You see?" he says, barely turning back toward Gwen, whose face still seems stuck in the previous moment. "Didn't I tell you he would be here? This is the place. The place we need to be."

"Get me out of this place," she says quietly. "I will not bring the boys here. Look at me, Jack."

But he doesn't. He puts one twitching finger on my arm, starts talking, keeps talking.

"Stopped by your house, left our little guys with your lovely wife and some alpha chick. There were cookies everywhere. Your little Spring and my two guys gobbled them up, covered in cookie crumbs, laughing. Well, Spring was laughing. My two don't. They don't laugh much lately."

"They laugh just as much as they ever laughed," Gwen says. "They do."

Jack is swaying now, like he's on a sailboat buffeted by wind. "They have to come here. I think so. We need answers. Or I don't know what will happen. Gwen wanted to see. To see what the doctor does here. So he showed us. We saw a boy. Down that corridor. Go take a look. You ought to take a look. A boy. Being treated. *Pressing down on him the weight of selfhood.* That's what Dr. Grunwald says. Amazing. Fascinating. He's not being crushed. He's not being harmed, Gwen. No. Grounded. He's being grounded."

Jack looks awful. The word *distraught* hangs in the air over his head. I've seen that face before, only it was my face then. The incident. Spring almost leaving us. I look away. Dr. Maire seems to be engaged in some sort of Germanic two-step with Dr. Grunwald, each clamping a hand on the other's shoulder, muttering darkly.

Up on the stucco wall, the painting stares down at me and the figures seem to be moving, too, as if part of some Dadd anime. I blink, shake the slightest chill from my neck, and the radiant men, the thin ax-wielder, they are all standing still again, just there in the painting, motionless, as they should be.

As am I.

There's a tightness in my chest; I've felt this before, but never so strong. I think of my father dropping dead that morning out of the blue.

"I need to get home," I say to no one in particular.

Grunwald breaks his pose, sidles toward us. Dr. Maire strokes his sharp chin, abstracted again. He takes off his glasses, wipes them with a handkerchief. He seems to be in some sort of pain, his stick-like frame bending toward the floor. He looks up at the painting, looks anywhere but at me.

"And so, the boys. Shall we send the van for them?" Grunwald says to Jack, as if this were a perfectly ordinary question. "As we discussed?"

Gwen strides across the room, the palms of her hands pushing the air before her. "There will be no van!" she shouts.

"Mrs. Donald, if I may," Grunwald says, all middle European formality. "Is it not the case that you too worry about little Henry and Edward? You did say, did you not, that you had noticed things, things that were not as they should be? That they do not play as they played a year ago, that they seem sometimes changed to you? Drifting somewhere, out into the ether, as if beckoned away? Yes, as if there had been some change in their being, some change of an essential thing, an essential truth? And the doubling of behavior, did you not mention this? So that when one twin wanders off into a dark place, the other follows? Yes, twins. Very difficult cases indeed sometimes. The folie à deux effect I described to you? And as I told you those things, did the thought not strike you that those things might be true, as I say they are true. Did you not think so, Mrs. Donald? Yes?"

Gwen is swaying now too, her pale face flushed.

"The Changeling Child. Trouble. But we will look, we will see, we will not do anything that is not called for. We will do nothing—or very little—that is not what might well be approved by those who know about matters of this nature, yes? Do we have your permission? Yes?"

"But the therapy? The pressing down therapy. Tell me again. Why?"

"To be grounded. Pressed to earth. Yes, to join the two halves and keep the one true self from slipping away, splitting into two, don't you see? To keep things as they should be, not as they could be. So do we have your permission? To try things that may perhaps need to be tried?"

"I don't know," she murmurs, and she looks up at Jack for help, but he has already leaped toward the door.

"I'll go with the van!" he shouts.

"No!" Grunwald barks. "The changelings must be alone."

"They're...they're only four," Gwen says.

"It is not their age that is a factor here, no. It is the depth. How far have they gone into that tunnel, and how quickly can we get them to emerge, hmm? Isn't that what we want?" He spins on his heel, gestures to the green-clad bouncer, who at the moment appears to be barring the door. "Get the van."

Then suddenly, *Spring falling through the air*—I can see her so clearly, and I feel numb panic grip my chest like it did that night, and I wonder what I would do if it were not Jack's little boys but my little girl the van was coming for, to take her away.

"I'll accompany your driver in the van," someone declares.

It is an unfamiliar voice but when I turn toward it, I see that it is Dr. Maire, no longer staring up at the painting but suddenly in the center of the room. He seems to have gotten some jolt of renewed energy. He is no longer wilting, appears instead to be tall and clear and calm.

"I am very good with children, as my son-in-law might tell you, and I know a shortcut to their place. Their place is…quite out of the way, wouldn't you say, Paul? But if I were to take the route we took before, wouldn't that be the better route for the van to take?"

"The route we took?"

I admit, I have no idea what he is getting at. He keeps shooting me little looks, little conspiratorial looks, and gesturing at his jacket pocket, as if he had some treasure there, some treasure that might change everything.

"You take my car, Paul," he says slowly. "I'll bet you want to get home to your lovely family, do you not? And have a word with them?"

He comes up behind me, beaming; he scoops something out of his pocket, some kind of canister or inhaler, which he jiggles before me, as if about to perform sleight of hand. No one else seems to be paying attention to us. "I will detain them, manipulate them. It can be done," he whispers. "I can do it."

I lift my head. It feels so heavy, but I nod. I say, "Yes, sure," and I take his keys, turn and walk down the corridor.

There are several rooms off the corridor, each with a thick metal door and the tiny slit of a window. I peer into the first room. The walls are pure white, like a video screen. I see images being projected onto the walls, familiar images. Scenes, characters, details all from *The Fairy Feller's Master-Stroke*, all flashing on the wall. And on the floor is a box and a little boy's head poking out of the box. It is Spring's friend Aidan, all tousled brown hair with the tiniest hint of green, like leaves or moss were woven there. And something all over his little body. Stones. Stones pressing down on him, and I wave to him, I don't know why, and he looks up, eyes grave and sad. Crying. He is crying, but there is no sound except my own constricted breathing.

Help me, he mouths.

I run down the hall, peer in the second door. The painting again, glowering over another narrow bed, and another boy—or is it the same boy?—buried beneath stones.

I feel dizzy. I am certain Grunwald and goon are about to descend on me, grab me, shove me in a box, place stones on my body. But when I glance back, I see that for a change no one is looking at me. They are looking at each other, Gwen staring pitifully up at Jack and Jack grinning nervously at Grunwald, who cocks his head at Dr. Maire, standing in the middle of the room almost militarily straight, as if on parade, while the bouncer boy hovers nearby with a huge ring of keys.

"Jack, you stay here," Dr. Maire suggests, as if he were a kindly old retainer. "You have a good long talk with my old friend Grunwald. Gwen, dear, you go with Paul. Why not have a chat with Nadia, hmm? Ask her about the boys. What she thinks of...their condition. Paul, go ahead. Take Gwen, help her through this little ordeal. I will come with the van for the boys. And we shall all see. What we shall see."

Jack nods. Gwen nods. Everyone nods.

"Well, then," Dr. Maire says. He looks down the hall at me, right at me. "Go!"

21.

"This can't…this can't happen," Gwen says.

"It won't," I say, as if soothing a child. I pat her hand, which is locked onto my arm like a blood pressure wristband. I ease her into Dr. Maire's ancient Volvo, yank on the safety belt, strap her in as if she were my child. She exhales sharp, hard breaths as we barrel down Pantherkill Road.

Or is that me?

I race through the door and Nadia gives me one of her puzzled looks. Dakota squints at me, clenches her jaw. But Spring leaps into my arms and I hug her, hug her as if I might lose her at any moment.

"Spring, honey, call the boys. We have to go. We have to go out," I say. "We have to get them away. Right now."

Gwen staggers along behind me, dazed. She seems to be thinking about all this but unable to act—the way I am, usually, but not today, I don't know why, not today.

"What's going on?" Nadia says, and she looks like she might cry, like her worst fears might be taking shape before her beautiful green eyes.

I don't let go of Spring; I won't let go of her. I spin her in my arms around the room. "Your father told me to take them, to take the boys away, hide them," I say, trying to sound reasonable.

"What?" Gwen says. Her hypnotized eyes suddenly flicker.

"The van is right behind us."

"What van?" Dakota demands, but I step past her and grab Nadia's arm with my free hand.

"They're going to hurt these boys in the name of helping them; that's what your father thinks."

"What?" Gwen says.

"You're quoting my father to me," Nadia sighs. "You know I hate that."

"Okay, I do know that. But I think he's right this time. Trouble...but Spring can help me, she can help me with the boys. Call to them, honey," I tell her, "Call them away."

"Where is Jack?" Nadia asks. "Gwen, what do you want to do with the boys?"

"I...I..."

"Call them, sweetie," I say to Spring, who begins to sing.

And it's just a box of rain, I don't know who put it there, she bellows. I hold her high above my head, gazing up at the glorious in-the-moment-ness of her. She waves her tiny hands in the air like a conductor and does just what I wanted her to do; she sings, she sings to the boys, she calls to the boys, and they are sitting there at the kitchen table, little blond elves with blank eyes and they look up, look right at her, suddenly all alert, and they smile at her, they begin to dance a little, they follow us, they follow her.

"Paul, you're scaring me," Nadia whispers. But it's too late to go back now. She'll see. She'll believe in me again.

We all dance through the yard, past the unsuccessful herb garden and the apple tree which seems dead every winter but isn't, and the frail red maple sapling, and the huge old pine tree all but denuded of its branches last March that stares down at us gravely like some ancient totem pole. All these places where I've watched Spring run and bounce and roll around and I've never noticed how beautiful how radiant they are for that, for her presence, for her five-year-old aliveness.

How beautiful my life is with her in it. How dark it will be—would be, would be—if she were to leave.

Or if I were.

If I were to continue to feel this tightness in my chest, for example, or this puzzling vertigo I am struggling not to feel.

Out in the far corner of the yard, near the accursed swing set, where Dr. Maire said we should build a maze, I see that there *is* a sort of maze, that the dense bushes and overgrown brambles and big bobbing ferns and snaky twisted vines all make up a sort of passageway, that's what it looks like to me right now, a sort of green tunnel, like the one the Green Children of Woolpit must have wandered through.

Are we heading into the maze?

We are heading into the maze.

We head in, weaving like cats, first this way, then that way, and I am holding Spring's hand and she is holding one of the twins' hands and he holds his brother's hand, and I am leading them through the snarled greenery that is at the edge of the woods near the creek. I am the Pied Piper. No, Spring is. She is still singing, and the boys would follow her anywhere.

Anywhere.

Such a long long time to be gone and a short time to be there, she warbles and they seem to be singing too, and I hear another voice, Nadia's voice, calling to me, trying to call me back but I cannot go back right now. I have to lead these children to safety.

But is it safe? I see how overgrown it is in the woods ahead, how close it is to the edge of the creek, and I wonder if this tunnel is leading to some dark place, some place we shouldn't go, some place where children do not return from, and now I see the girl running up ahead of us, the green girl, who is calling to them, maybe she is the one who they—we—are all following.

Maybe I should stop. Maybe I should stop them.

I stop. I am panting. I am sweating. "Spring, honey," I gasp. "Is that...is that your friend up there?"

Spring looks back at me but I do not recognize her eyes; they seem blank, gone, and she hurtles forward into the woods, the boys trailing behind her.

I feel something, a twinge. I look down at myself, my soon-to-be-useless body. No, I do not wish to feel this twinge. No, I do not think I will acknowledge this twinge. Spring is far ahead, the green girl dancing in front of her, in front of them. There are four of them and they are all green and they are all a blur and they are all headed toward the thicket at the edge of the creek, and they are all gone, and I am gone, no I am not, the pain is not gone, the pain is yet to come and I feel it shooting down my left side, and I say, "Wait, wait for me," or try to say it. "Don't go, Spring, don't go, don't go," I am chanting now or think I am. I am on the ground, looking up at someone's face, someone's beautiful face. Nadia's face, and it is she who is saying those words: Don't go, don't go, Paul, she says—no, that's not right. She's saying, *don't die, no, don't die, no.*

No.

22.

The trouble is not now...the trouble is yet to...

No, it's now. The trouble is now, and I am in it. It's like a funnel cloud, and I am spinning, spinning.

No, I am not.

I am lying down, splayed out on the green, green grass and it's damp after some late afternoon thunderstorm that is rolling over me that has me that is me. I am in the storm. I am the storm.

No, I am not.

I can't move. My head throbs. I am curled up in pain on familiar/unfamiliar ground. I am paralyzed. But I am not. I lift my head. But I don't.

No. None of that is right, none of that is true. There is only one truth, and it is that I...I am running. Running after Spring, who is holding the twins' little hands, and they are all running after the green girl. We are running together, all five of us, and we cannot stop.

I cannot stop.

Spring is ahead, so far ahead, and I need to catch hold of her. The boys dance and prance around her, wild with delight at their escape, but I need to catch up to Spring. To hold her, to make her stay.

I am the only one who can.

But I can't.

Because I am sitting down on the damp ground, rocking back and forth like I used to when I was a boy and my father was angry at me, which was pretty much all the time.

There is someone, a girl. It is not my mother, it is not my wife, it is not my daughter. She is standing—no, hovering beside me. Looking at me, arms crossed, eyes fixed on the ground. The green girl.

"Agnes?" I whisper.

"You know my name. How?"

"My daughter."

"Who?"

"Spring."

She turns from me, so that all I can see is the back of her head, the little shells of her mossy ears. "Spring is not yours."

I laugh. I am laughing, though it sounds far away, as if someone else were laughing eons ago, miles from here.

"Oh, she is mine all right," I say. "When I see her, I smile or cry or fall down. Like a needle in my heart, I feel her there all the time, the pain of her, the wonderful horrible pain of her. I feel her weight on my shoulders, on my thoughts every day, every night, every moment."

"Oh."

She is looking far off to a field I had not noticed before, where Spring and the boys canter, my daughter's wispy black hair fluttering in the breeze.

"She doesn't belong to you. To your world," Agnes says firmly, her little greenish chin jutting toward me. Her voice is high and thin, the mere suggestion of a sound. "She belongs to my world. My. World."

"That is not true," I shout or think I am shouting, though no sound comes from my clenched mouth.

"Why do you want her to be a part of your world?" she asks. She says the word *your* as if it were a curse. "So full of sorrow and danger. Things die there. Nothing lasts there. In my world, the sorrow is over. Gone. There is no light to torment you—always ahead of you, never on you. There is no falling or hurting there. The fall is over, the hurt is past. Know what we call it? St. Martin's Land. Isn't that pretty? Isn't that the name of a place where Spring could always always be? There is no crying in St. Martin's Land. There is no sound at all, just the green darkness that comes of closing your eyes your ears your mouth your heart. Shall I take her there? Come away, little Spring, I shall say to her. Come away to a place where no one can be harmed. You may bring your little friends too, to the place where no mother or father can look at you and say, what is wrong with my child? For there, nothing is wrong and that is the place where we shall go."

"No," I cry out. "No, please do not take her. Please do not take her. Take me instead, take me instead..."

Agnes puts her tiny hands on her hips. "You want her to feel pain?" she asks, incredulous.

"If I could keep her from feeling pain but let her feel all the rest I would. But they're all bound up in a big messy package. Let her have it—the whole package. Let her live. Let her live in the world. I never could."

"But you do. You do. And you want this for her?"

I sigh. I sit down. No, I am already sitting. I am sitting with my legs crossed, my arms crossed, holding myself together, and I am crying, huge blobby tears running down my cheeks. "Oh, if I could only keep her from all the pain of this world," I sob.

"But you can't," Agnes whispers in my ear. "Can't can't can't. So let the Beautiful Little One come with me. Come away, little Spring."

I am standing. Suddenly I am standing though my whole body aches. But I must move, I must get going, I must reach Spring, tell her not to look at this girl, not to look too closely at this girl this Agnes this changeling this green child from some world we don't see inside the world we live in.

But Spring is gone.

No, she is not.

She is here, right beside me, kneeling on her little knees, touching my sweaty forehead with one tiny finger.

"Did you fall down, Daddy? Are you okay?"

The two little boys stand behind her like baby ducklings waiting to be imprinted.

I smile. I try to smile anyway, but my mouth won't move. Nothing moves. I am flat, stiff, lifeless on the muddy ground.

Agnes dances all around us, waving her arms, buzzing like an insect child. There is the sound of her, the drone of her, like wings and legs rubbed together on a hot summer day.

The trouble is not now...

But it is. It is now.

"Come away, little Spring. Come away, oh human child. Come away with me to where there is no..."

"No," Spring says.

Agnes stops the buzzing for a moment, then starts again, weaving through the air around us like a mantis. "Come away, little Spring, to where there is no..."

"No! Want to stay here. With my daddy. Not going anywhere with you. Not with you." She grabs the little boys and holds them to her. "We are staying, aren't we? We are."

Agnes squints at her with one greenish eye. She begins again. "Come away, little Spring, to dark green lovely inside world, friends and fairies and a beautiful shiny ax and a carriage made out of a hazelnut and so, so much more. Not here. Too much pain and sorrow here. Come away, little Spring, where there will be no…"

"No. I said no. Daddy needs me to be here. I need him to be here. I want to be here." She leaps up, high into the air. She calls out. "Mommy, Mommy, come help me get Daddy up. Daddy needs help, come help. Help! Help!"

And that sound—*help, help, help*, her little voice, her little yelp—is all I can hear or see or feel until other hands touch me.

Such a long long time to be gone…

There are hands, so many of them, and they are reaching out to me, touching me, pulling me back into somewhere, away from the gray-green darkness.

23.

It is not my father. But somebody's father.

It is not my father who is picking me up. Picking me up off the damp lawn where I have been lying for...days? Hours? Minutes?

It is not my father. I know that, I know that. My father has been dead since I was twenty-four, though Nadia likes to say I still carry him around with me, that I talk about him more than she talks about her own father, who is very much still with us.

Still with us. With me.

Nadia.

Her father.

Dr. Maire.

He is carrying me. Dr. Maire is carrying me, and Spring is standing there, jumping up and down, giggling.

"Look," she crows. "Look, Pop-Pop is carrying Daddy!"

But is it a giggle? Is it not more like a howl? That's the kind of distinction I always have a hard time making, even when I'm being carried, even when I'm in the nonsensical position of being carried by a man who is a generation older than me, a bony bird of a man but he's carrying me anyway, holding my stiff body like Lear holding Cordelia and I would surely laugh if I could.

I can.

I can laugh, more or less.

"He's laughing!" Spring reports. "Mommy! Daddy is okay! He's laughing!" and she sprints across the yard toward Nadia, who is not laughing, who looks awful, like she's been crying. Is still crying.

I'm inside now. Inside our house. Our house, which I will not leave, which I refuse to leave ever again. I am lying on the couch where Dr. Maire slept just this morning—was it this morning? Was it not a year ago?

Time. It's frozen again. Like the painting, my painting, the ax frozen forever just before it strikes. That's how it feels to me now that I am lying down on our couch and Spring is sitting here holding my hand, lightly, gently, like she's afraid to press too hard.

Gwen is hugging her twins, holding them tightly the way Spring was holding them. They are motionlessly poised to get away from her, their little mouths open as if to screech, though there is no sound.

"I have dispatched the van man," Dr. Maire says cryptically. "I have immobilized Grunwald and his minion with a dollop of shamanic arts. No more trouble from Grunwald."

Dakota has the phone. She's holding onto it, her big arm frozen in midair. No, now she's moving it, gesturing with it. There is time, there is movement, the ax swings again. Suddenly the boys shriek in the background—or suddenly I hear it anyway—followed by Gwen quieting them over and over, like the whoosh of a sprinkler.

"Do we think he had a stroke?" Dakota asks, waving her arm above her head, as if signaling to someone I cannot see. "Nadia, they're asking me, do we think he had a stroke?"

"How do I know?" Nadia wails. "We need to get him to the emergency room!"

"No," I croak. "I'm okay." But I can hear my voice and it doesn't sound okay.

"You are not okay, my boy," Dr. Maire confirms. "Someone needs to take a look at you. Someone who has more than a degree in metaphysics or infant care." He gestures dismissively toward Dakota, which almost makes me smile. If I could smile.

I can. I can smile.

"Daddy is smiling! Agnes went away, Daddy. Are you glad I didn't go with her?"

This is what I think she says, anyway; I nod weakly.

Nadia sits down next to me, practically shoving her father to the floor. "What if it happens again? Whatever it was. We need to get you to a hospital," she says.

"I hate hospitals."

"Unlike the rest of us, who love them," Nadia says. "Does Margaretville even have an emergency room?"

"I don't need an emergency room. The emergency is over. The trouble is…over." And for the first time I can say that. Feel that.

But Nadia can't feel it. Her face, her hands, her blouse, all are wet with tears. "I was so scared. You fell. Like a tree. Like something cut you down. We have to see somebody. Now!"

And I have not seen such a tight, pained look on her beautiful face since that day in the hospital chapel after Spring's incident, when I wanted my own life to end right there just to avoid the pain I was feeling. So, I need to fix this; I need to agree to something.

"Okay, okay." I sigh. "Phone that quack Balin. He makes house calls. The last doctor on earth to make house calls."

She leaps up, grabs the phone from Dakota.

"That guy?" Dakota says. "We want that guy?"

"We want somebody," Nadia snaps, and then strides off into the living room, whispering frantically into the phone.

24.

"So what is the deal, Paul?" was all he said.

Time must have passed, screeches must have been screeched and shushes shushed and Dr. Maire must have posed rhetorical questions and Dakota must have dithered and Nadia must have cried and Spring must have giggled and leaped around and kissed me and held my hand, but I don't recall any of that.

Then Dr. Balin was standing here, musing. He looked me over, first from this side, then from that side, looked at me longer than anyone has ever looked at me, except two of my three wives maybe (I don't recall Laura, my first wife, ever really looking at me). Not a medical examination kind of look, exactly, though he was nibbling on his lip the way I do sometimes when I'm trying to figure something out.

He did do the examination thing, the stethoscope, the peering into eyes, the blood pressure thing, about thirty seconds worth of that stuff, then five minutes, the longest five minutes in history, just looking at me, shifting on the edge of the chair Nadia had pushed next to the couch, squinting one eye, then the other, at me, at my life as I lay collapsed into myself on the couch.

Then he banished everyone else. Even Nadia, though she hovered in the doorway, wondering, like I was, what the hell he was doing. The others were all herded into the kitchen. I could hear the boys yowling and I heard Spring, too, heard her call to them, coo to them, their new friend and protector.

Dr. Maire refused to leave the room at first—he's used to being consulted on all manner of things he actually knows nothing about, so maybe he was hoping. "Dr. Balin," he mused, "have you ever heard of a *fairy stroke*? The invisible hand seizing us? Flinging us down?"

"I think we'll leave the invisible world out of this for now," Balin said, nudging him toward the door. "We have enough trouble coming at us from the visible one."

Now it's just the two of us. I raise myself up on one shaky elbow. "You should probably know...I should tell you..."

"Tell me," he says.

"My father had a heart attack. Died. When he was my age, just about."

"But that isn't all, is it? You saw something, were afraid of something. That's what everyone seems to be telling me. *Like you saw a ghost*, is what your wife said."

I exhale loudly. "Not a ghost. Something small. Dark. Calling Spring, calling her away. Spring...I was afraid...afraid of losing her, afraid she would leave us, afraid she would be... carried away by...by..." I couldn't say the words *a green girl. A changeling child.* I couldn't form the words, or didn't want to.

Dr. Balin nods, as if he knows what I am talking about. "Do you know that poem by Goethe? *Who rides so late through the night and wind?* The evil Elf King who takes the little boy from his father? I don't have kids. Always thought I would, but it didn't work out. Married twice; it never even came up in conversation. Still I can imagine, I think I can, how it's always there, that fear, the night rider who will whisk the child into darkness. You can call it whatever you like. Fever. Magic. Pervasive Developmental Delay. So, sure, maybe you saw something. There are things we see sometimes, even if nobody else sees them. Flash of light? A hand reaching out? Flash of pain? Then you fell down? I'm thinking pre-aortic aura, the visual thing, the hallucination, let's call it. Sure, a mild heart attack. I'm thinking that's what we're going to find when we get you some tests."

"But I don't want tests."

"Who does?"

"I want to stay here...I need to be with Nadia and Spring."

"Yes, you do." He stands up, stretches. "Such a long, long time to be gone and a short time to be there," he sighs.

"What?"

"Just a song that's in my head."

"That was the song...that was the song I heard, as I was falling..."

"We probably listen to the same radio station." He closes his bag. He actually has one of those black doctor bags you see on old TV shows. "Do you want me to drive you down to Kingston, or do you want your wife to do it? We need some tests," he adds, with a stony expression that suggests no room for argument.

I am still propped up on one elbow. I want to argue, to argue that the best thing I could do would be nothing, which is what I always want to argue.

"It was like a dream. The past few days were like a dream. What I saw, what I thought I saw wasn't real...was it? So why do I have to do real things to take care of it?"

"The pain was real, though, wasn't it? And you lost consciousness. You didn't dream that."

"But..."

He holds up his hand like a traffic cop. "Let's stop. Let's not go there. What matters are your wife and kid and keeping you here, okay?"

"Okay," I mutter.

"I'll call Benedictine, we can all go down together. A little healthcare outing."

But as he strides to the door, I hear more voices, doors slamming, and Nadia runs in, holding her head like it might explode, followed by her father, followed by Jack, followed by an unsteady Grunwald, followed by the green-clad bouncer, who appears to have just awakened.

"Oh Lord," Dr. Balin says. "What the hell are they doing here?"

"Oooof," the bouncer groans. "Head hurts."

"Did you think your little voodoo tricks would keep us away, old friend, old foe? Did you?" Grunwald demands.

"Do not like that man!" Spring cries out, and the boys wail, and Gwen shouts Jack's name, and everyone is yelling and waving.

Dr. Maire stretches his arms out, like Moses at the Red Sea. But nothing happens, except for his teeth clamping together and the sweat breaking out on his forehead.

"The boys," Grunwald demands, stretching out his stubby arm. "I've come for the boys."

25.

"I can't believe I didn't notice before how much Grunwald looks like the old gnome in the painting!" I blurted to Dr. Maire after the tumult died down. He gave me a slightly pained look, jiggling his hands in the air in a *not now* sort of gesture.

But it's true. A hawk-like nose, an unruly hedge of a beard, an outstretched hand, as if signaling to someone. And when he took off his glasses—as he did after Gwen took a swing at him—his eyes seemed to be spinning in his head, just as the creepy old man's eyes seem to be spinning in the painting.

Maybe I'm off the mark here—it wouldn't be the first time—but I saw it. For a moment I saw what it was in the Dadd painting that made it fit so perfectly on the wall of the Grunwald Center: a cold zeal, detached obsession, insect-like repetitive drone in place of actual feeling.

"I don't think I can ever look at that painting again," I told Nadia on the way down to Benedictine Hospital, but she didn't respond. Possibly, just possibly, I didn't actually say it. Maybe I only thought it, or I murmured it along with all the other things I was murmuring. Maybe she didn't hear me. Or didn't believe me.

Well, I've made sweeping statements previously about trying to keep my little pet obsessions closer to the realm of the normal—whatever that may be—and maybe Nadia feels like I haven't kept those promises. Something like that.

Or maybe she was just musing on all the other, somewhat less focused things I had said in the past few hours.

Because that was after I yelled at Jack, yelled at everyone, told them what I had seen as I was leaving the Center, told them how that painting hovered over little Aidan and how the little boy was pressed down, crying out in the darkness, and how those images hovered on every wall in every room. Which was around the time I threw up, too, thinking about Aidan and the pain being inflicted in that place, about the pain that might be inflicted on Spring, or on the twins. On any child. Every child.

And it was right then—an unfrozen moment if ever there was one—that Jack turned to Gwen and said, "The boys are going to the Center." Said it calmly, firmly, as if, in spite of my warning, there could be no dispute. Except there was a dispute, there was Gwen suddenly whirling around, eyes flashing.

"The hell they are, you asshole! Are you out of your fucking mind, Jack?" she snapped.

That was when she took a swing at Grunwald, who, to my surprise, was quite adept at ducking, as if maybe he had plenty of practice doing this. And then Gwen, her face red, added, "And if you want to ever see them again, I recommend you come home with me. Now."

Jack blushed, his eternally tan face tinged with scarlet. He shrugged. I'm usually the one who shrugs, who is uncertain. But not this time. "Okay. Sure," he murmured. "You win. The boys go home."

"But...but...but," Grunwald sputtered. It was like in a Roadrunner cartoon, where you see steam coming out of the coyote's ears. "Do you not see that we must seize the changelings? Seize them to save them? There is no time! No time for doubt! Do you wish to be left with the empty husks of your children? The shadows of your twins? No! No, you do not! But if we fail to infuse them with the truth of selfhood, that is all, that is all we shall have of them! Surely…surely you see this?"

The air in the living room was thick with unscreamed words. I sat up on the couch; this was almost as exciting as green children wandering up out of a secret land.

Dr. Maire and Dr. Balin glared at Grunwald, as if they could make him disappear with the force of their disapproval.

"Now! We must act now!"

Grunwald stormed toward the twins, his meaty hand reaching out as if to grab them by the scruff of their necks, like kittens. But Nadia and Dakota and Gwen circled the children with linked arms, a stone-faced wall of common sense.

"Get out of my house," Nadia said. "You heard their mother. They are not going with you. Anywhere. Ever."

Was the old man going to fly into a rage? Flail against the wall of women?

No. He wilted, shrank like a balloon leaking air. "We cannot split the one into two…" he began. But Dr. Maire cut him off.

"You should be so ashamed!" is all he said. He jerked his head toward the door, and without another word Grunwald and his goon slunk out, like defeated warriors.

Gwen glided toward Nadia; they hugged. There was a lot of hugging going on, though I was not part of it. Then she grabbed her boys, scooping up Spring with her free arm. "You are so brave and so full of life. I want my boys to be just like you," she whispered hoarsely into Spring's lovely seashell ear. "Will you be their buddy?"

Spring giggled, hugged her back. "That would be so fun," she said, and the twins clutched her legs, and Jack stood there, shifting his weight from one foot to the other, grinning like the idiot he had recently revealed himself to be.

He waved to me, as if he didn't want to get too close. "Feel better, Brickner, old pal. We'll get the kids together soon, am I right, Nadia…?"

"It's been taken care of, Jack," Gwen said, and they shuffled out of our house, which seemed almost normal again.

Almost.

Dakota's continued presence, looming behind Nadia like a denim-clad mountain, was not quite the norm. "I should have been the one to step in, to stop her from racing off with those boys. I'm her godmother," she muttered darkly. "And what did I do? Diddly!"

Spring thought this was hilarious. She shouted the word *diddly* over and over like a mantra. That's pretty normal, I think. And she did not look green, and there were no changeling children darting around the periphery of my vision.

That has to be good.

But Nadia's fretfulness, that was not the norm—not the norm at all. She leaped back and forth, first smoothing Spring's wispy hair, then stroking my damp forehead; she was jittery, almost as if she were channeling me while I sat quiet and calm on the couch, the way she usually does.

And Dr. Balin. What was he doing here again? And why did my left arm ache? Why did I feel as if I had recently crumpled over and was barely uncrumpled?

He turned toward me. "Let's get you down to Kingston, get you looked at," he said, a little too loudly.

"Oh," I said.

And I remembered.

"Okay," I said.

I remembered Agnes whispering, *Come away, come away,* and Spring saying, *No, no, my daddy needs me here. I need him here.*

I grabbed Spring and held her like she might still be yanked away from me at any moment. The sweet clover smell of her hair, the palpable feel of her in my arms—and how I could have lost that, could still lose it, was doomed to go through my life fearing I might lose it, that almost knocked me out all over again.

And that's when I started to cry, I think, and then seeing me all wrought up, Nadia started to cry, so I stopped, I took a breath, I held my breath, I let it out slowly. "Sure, Doc. Let's hit the road."

So we did.

26.

In college I once found Tommy sprawled out on the steps of the library, flipping through a large, rectangular, purple book called *Be Here Now*. Most of his reading consisted of back issues of *Rolling Stone*, *High Times*, and sci-fi paperbacks about cosmic conspiracies; he knew I would shrink from those as from a leper, so he never thrust them on me. But he was always trying to get me to read *Be Here Now*.

"Listen to this, Paul," he would declare. "*The next message you need is always right where you are.* I'm telling you, you have to read this thing."

"I've never been *here now* or any other time," I said.

And that pretty much remains true, although today I have promised Nadia that I will do my best. Usually my best falls far short of the mark, and I end up yelling go fuck yourself at people who (apparently) mean me no harm, but not today. Today is for Spring. Today is Dad Low Day. This is what Spring tells me.

I think she means *Tableau Day*. That's what Miss Tania called it a few weeks ago, though that seems remarkably pompous for a preschool graduation. *Dad Low Day* sounds about right.

"June 21 is a very big day in my life, Daddy!" my little elf declared to me last night. "All us kids wear cool costumes and dance and sing and say stuff, and you have to promise to be there with me and to be happy, happy, happy."

So that's two promises I've made about this day.

For reasons not entirely clear, Spring's preschool graduation is all wrapped up in a dance recital and family outing at Puck's Hill Nursery School, where we will munch on organic chicken nuggets, carrot sticks, and frozen yogurt (these items were specifically mentioned on the flyer) and watch our little ones perform Miss Tania's elaborate pantomime.

Puck's Hill is dotted with colorful blankets and beach towels, like some polite rock concert, where moms and dads and siblings and family friends and even a couple of dogs and one ferret are lolling in the midday sun. There are several goldfinches flitting about, a lone redwing blackbird perched on the fence, and some strange blue butterflies I've never seen before.

"Did you notice those butterflies?" I ask, as we smooth Nadia's old faded army blanket on the grass for the picnic.

Nadia nods. "Yes, I noticed them," she says, perhaps more emphatically than necessary.

It is a thoroughly fine first day of summer. Tiger lilies bounce their big orange heads along the back fence, and little wild violets embroider the field. Nadia is holding my hand so tightly I'm afraid she might draw blood.

"You're okay, right?" she asks.

I smile inscrutably. Nadia has been so worried about my health—I'm fine, by the way, fine—that I worry more about her worrying about me than anything else. This is an additional reason for my thoughts to drift and for me to fail to be here now, but I am working on it. I am working on it. I wave jauntily to the approaching figure of Miss Tania. "Miss Tania thinks you don't exist, by the way," I tell Nadia.

"But I do." She leans in and kisses me. She has been so attentive to me since Dr. Balin's predictions proved true— "See!" he announced, showing us my chart. "Minor infarction. Could be worse!"—that in another lifetime I might have been put off. But I am pleased now to have this lifetime, frayed though it might be, to have, as Freud suggested, normal human unhappiness.

I am trying to notice everything today, everything around me, and trying not to see—or fear that I might see— green girls. I am trying not to suspect—for the time being anyway—that there are visitors from a world inside our world skittering around Puck's Hill. I am hoping that this day will offer nothing more mysterious than Miss Tania's clownish grin as she bounds toward our blanket.

"Mr. B, so glad, so glad. And this is the mythical Mom?"

Nadia, who is usually far better than I am at feigning politesse, can barely force a sliver of her gorgeous smile. She shakes Miss Tania's outstretched hand. "I can't believe my Spring is graduating from preschool today," she says, because it's the sort of thing you say. "My baby is growing up."

"Oh, they are not really ours, are they?" Miss Tania intones, in her strange clipped accent. She pats the back of her head with one hand while gesturing to one of her assistants with the other. "They are all on loan, are they not? And then *pffft*. Gone. But wait until you see our little masque. Art and truth and magic all rolled up into one happy package!" She pivots, as if called by an unheard signal, striding toward the next gaggle of grown-ups.

"What a horrible person," Nadia says. But then she leaps up. "Dad!" she cries out, far happier to see him than usual.

Since he was, perhaps inadvertently, one of the heroes of my little altercation with life, Dr. Maire has been welcomed by Nadia as if all of the wounds of the past have been washed away.

He meanders toward us, intently staring at a large book. Behind him are Gwen and the two little boys, both wearing white shorts and tiny seersucker jackets. But no Jack. Jack has been off somewhere—Thailand, I think—finding himself. I do wonder what he'll find when he finds himself.

"Paul, my boy," Dr. Maire says, virtually ignoring his daughter as usual. "Thought you might like this book." He thrusts it at me. *Outsider Art: From Dadd to Darger.* I almost drop it.

I think about Tommy, can see him staring at the pages. I think about my father. Both gone too soon. But I am still here. Need to stay here. Will stay here.

"Knew the author once, long ago," he continues. "But that was in another country. This is the sort of book you could write, my boy. Were you not thinking about such a thing?"

"I'm just thinking about Spring today," I say. "Trying to stay focused on her."

"Yes, yes, of course," he murmurs. He absently hugs Nadia, lowers himself onto the blanket. "But do you know the one thing these outsider artists had in common? Do you?"

I do not, and right now I do not care. Gwen and Nadia are leaning in, whispering and laughing; Gwen has produced a bottle of wine and is pouring it into paper cups while Henry and Edward spin wildly around the periphery of the blanket. "Where is Spring? Where is Spring?" they chant. Gwen gives them each a pat on the head.

"They're doing so well," Nadia says. And maybe they are. I'm trying to see it that way. I'm trying to look at what's there instead of what could be there.

Unfortunately, what's there at the moment is Miss Tania, now standing in the center of the hill, holding aloft a flute.

"My dear, dear friends," she begins.

"Dreams, my boy. Dreams which leaked out into their conscious world," Dr. Maire stage-whispers to me. I nod, as if considering this observation. He takes the plastic cup Nadia offers him and drains it in a single gulp.

"It is the first day of summer and the last day of our little school," Miss Tania declaims. "Let the gala masque begin!"

27.

Miss Tania tootles on the flute, making little insect twittering sounds. There is an electronic wave of music from the building behind us, and out onto the walkway march thirteen little boys and girls. They are holding hands. Carefully, carefully, they lift their bare little feet and weave across Puck's Hill. They are wearing shiny pink and purple and yellow and green and blue tunics.

They are ridiculous. They are adorable. Spring, in a green satiny number, grins and bounces at the head of the line of children. She dances forward.

Come unto these yellow sands, she says in her sweet, piping voice, *and then take hands.*

The little band of preschool fairies grasp one another's small, moist hands. They spin and wave their arms; the boy in blue stumbles, the girl in pink stops, looks scared, but Spring comes up behind her, touches her lightly on her cardboard wings, and she dances on.

The flute is still keening away but there is another sound— what is that other sound? A jangling hum in my ears. No, it's nothing, just the sound of summer, the buzzing, the ticking, the distant thrum of traffic on Route 28.

Be not afeard. The isle is full of noises, the little boy in purple bellows. The fairy children grasp hands again and run madly in a circle across the top of the hill.

Sometimes a thousand twangling instruments will hum about mine ears, and sometime voices, shouts a tiny, familiar voice.

"Oh my God," Nadia says. "She really does look like a little enchanted creature, doesn't she?" She stands up, yanks out her camera, begins snapping pictures. Once again I am profoundly grateful for her down-to-earth ways. She is not transfixed or terrified or appalled by the sight of our daughter behaving like a being from one of my bad dreams; she wants to record it, freeze this moment in time.

I shiver, though it is steamy and airless on Puck's Hill. I have seen so many moments frozen, moments that I wished would unfreeze. But not this one. Spring, lovely and joyous—oh how I would freeze this moment forever if I could.

But I can't. She dances on, and will dance on.

One of the children is sitting down now, crying. The little girl in yellow has drifted off toward the shack where the hard-scrabble horses are kept. Still Spring and most of the others twirl and spin to the flute. There is a drum, too, somewhere far away. It sounds like one of those small Indian drums Tommy used to play sometimes, and it is echoing, echoing in my head.

No, it's not. It's just a drum. Just an accompaniment to this strange moment in time.

Dr. Maire pokes me in the arm. "How are you feeling, my boy? You look a little pale."

Miss Tania rises now, her somewhat frizzed-out red hair blowing in the summer breeze. She stands behind the gaggle of children. She places one hand on Spring's shoulder.

Up and down up and down I will lead them up and down I am fear'd in field and town Goblin lead them up and down, she chants.

She is looking right at me, through me.

No, she is not. She is just the annoying director of Spring's little nursery school, full of pomp and pretension and good intentions and nothing more, nothing more.

"This is all perfect," Gwen says. "The way things should be!"

Nadia sits, squeezes my hand. Do I look pale? Do I look like I've seen something that no one else sees? No, I am fine. I cast my gaze over to the huge old oak at the crest of the hill, and out of the corner of one eye I see a little girl, greenish, dashing around and around the tree.

"Did you see that?" Dr. Maire blares.

But it isn't. It isn't her. It's Spring. She climbs up the tree. *Oh Jesus,* I think. *Please…the trouble…no.*

But she stops at the first low branch. Miss Tania points to her with her flute. She swings down, little monkey that she is, crying out, *Shall we their fond pageant see? Lord, what fools these mortals be!*

All of the little gossamer kids join her now; she hops down, they hold hands, they take a bow. And the audience goes wild, and I go wild, cheering, wiping tears away with my sweaty sleeve, sighing, laughing. I hug Nadia, I hug Gwen. I even hug Dr. Maire.

"Did you see what I saw?" Dr. Maire asks me. But I don't answer.

The children race across the field, leaping onto blankets and into arms. Miss Tania bows low, then lifts her long arms above her head, like an athlete who has won a race.

Spring is hugging and being hugged. I step back, just to see her, just to see the tangible solidity of her tiny little frame.

"Daddy, Daddy, did you love what we did? Did you, Daddy?" she asks, grabbing onto my leg.

I lift her up. I look at her little dark eyes, flashing like every star in the sky. I kiss her forehead. I can't speak. Just for a moment. I am gasping for air. Just for a moment.

"I did," I say. "I really, truly did."

Several early and/or slightly edited versions of sections of *Come Away* appeared in *Third Wednesday* (Spring 2012), *Kindling Quarterly* (Summer 2014), and *Provincetown Arts* (Summer 2014). Thanks to David Perez and Chris Busa for their interest in my work. Thanks also to Lucy Appert and Robin Goldfin for their counsel, and to Global Liberal Studies at NYU for their support.

Richard Dadd was a real, semi-famous painter, and his masterpiece does indeed hang in the Tate. He also wrote a poem about the painting which makes, let us say, not a lot of sense. I substituted my own words for his poem to better connect it to the narrator's dark fears.